WHERE THE HEART IS

Malta 1968: Sylvana Bonnici's parents are dubious about her dream of being a globetrotting wife to British army staff sergeant Rob Denton. Sure enough, when Rob is posted to Singapore, the army dictates that he must leave her behind. When Rob is finally offered the posting Sylvana has yearned for, he's no longer sure that it's what he wants. Sylvana's reaction shocks him, but it's a horrifying accident that proves home is where the heart is . . .

SUE MOORCROFT

WHERE THE HEART IS

Complete and Unabridged

LINFORD
Leicester

First published in Great Britain in 2011

First Linford Edition
published 2013

British Library CIP Data

Moorcroft, Sue.
Where the heart is. - -
(Linford romance library)
1. Love stories.
2. Large type books.
I. Title II. Series
823.9'2–dc23

ISBN 978–1–4448–1506–1

Published by
F. A. Thorpe (Publishing)
Anstey, Leicestershire

Set by Words & Graphics Ltd.
Anstey, Leicestershire
Printed and bound in Great Britain by
T. J. International Ltd., Padstow, Cornwall

This book is printed on acid-free paper

1

1968

The fierce Maltese sun wouldn't set for another hour, but it was low enough to bleach the sky as Sylvana Bonnici hurried home from her job at the pharmacy on the Strand. Cars grumbled their way up Tower Road in busy Sliema, windows rolled down so that the occupants could catch the cooler air that evening brought.

It was June, and now the really hot weather was getting underway. Around her, the exodus from the workplace mingled with others setting out in the cool of the evening to meet friends and family; men in trousers and shirt sleeves, women in bright dresses, bouffant hair and lots of dark eye-liner.

Sylvana was not allowed to wear panda eye make-up at work and she'd call down the wrath of her father if she wore mini-skirts as short as some girls did, but her long dark hair was big and back-combed in a style she'd copied from a magazine and practised at home.

She was a big follower of the exciting Sixties fashions and the bright colours and zany patterns contrasted well with her dark colouring. She had only to note the number of male eyes that followed her progress to know that!

She almost skipped along the narrow pavement, saying, *'Scusi!'* or hopping off the kerb to let others pass, calling *'Ciao!'* when she saw a friend, without slackening her pace. She was caught up with a heart that was hopping and skipping, too.

It was really going to happen!

Around the next corner she'd meet Rob from his bus and . . .

'Sylvana!'

Suddenly there was a blond British soldier in front of her, immaculate in his khaki drill summer uniform along with his blue side hat and the badge of the Royal Signals bright upon it. 'Jimmy', the men called the little silver figure of Mercury. The three stripes on the khaki shirt sleeve with the crown above denoted the rank of staff sergeant, which he'd held for only a year.

'Rob!' Sylvana checked the slender silver watch that he had bought her for her birthday. 'Am I late?'

'I got off duty early — Martin swapped with me so I could. I've been so restless all day that I think he was glad to get rid of me!' His blue eyes laughed down at her. 'I'm nervous!'

Patting her heart, Sylvana pulled an agonised face.

'So am I! Mrs Sammut has scolded me all day for being in a dream.'

In uniform, Rob wouldn't try to link arms with her, but she kept a decorous distance anyway. If she was seen taking his arm in broad daylight the news would get home quicker than she could! The Bonnicis were well known in

3

Sliema and her parents were proud of their good name. That she had learned to love Rob so deeply in the scant year she'd known him wouldn't stop them expressing disapproval if they felt she wasn't behaving exactly as she ought.

Sylvana was the youngest of their four children, the only one left at home, and she knew what it was to be the focus of their attention.

Rob fell into step beside her.

'Let's get it over with, then,' he whispered. 'Crikey, I'm not this anxious facing my squadron commander when he's having a bad day.'

Maltese and English were the official languages of the Maltese Islands and a combination of both rose and fell around them as they walked. Conversation wasn't easy as they negotiated the human traffic, and they had mounted the hill and turned the corner before Robert spoke.

'What do you think he'll say?'

Sylvana grimaced as apprehension coiled and uncoiled in her stomach.

'Soon, we will find out! It is his half-day off from the restaurant today so he should be in a good mood. I hope.'

Butterflies

Turning left, they entered the grid of streets between Tower Road and Prince of Wales Road, twisting right and left between the limestone block houses lining the hot, dusty, narrow streets. The enclosed balconies or *gallerija* adorning the houses were painted in dark greens, reds and blues. Finally, the couple reached the flat-roofed house where Sylvana lived with her parents.

Two steps rose up from the pavement to the green front door with its inset of black wrought iron and the brass dolphin knocker that Sylvana's mother, Rita, polished twice a week.

Inside, they found Rita and Gwann about to leave for their evening walk. Rita's dark hair was swept back into a stylish chignon, much less flamboyant than Sylvana's beehive; Gwann was neat in a striped short-sleeved shirt.

Rita's eyebrows lifted fractionally.

'You have brought Robert. We are just leaving to meet Lino and Tereza and the children at the Magic Kiosk.'

Sylvana's family all spoke English. Gwann, working in the restaurant trade where English customers were common, had made sure of that.

Sylvana felt heat rush to her cheeks.

'We are just — ' she began.

'I was hoping — ' Rob said at the same time.

They hadn't even decided who would introduce the conversation that had flown around in Sylvana's head all day!

Rob gave her a reassuring grin before turning to Gwann.

'I was hoping to talk to you, sir. And to Mrs Bonnici.'

Gwann gazed at the tall young soldier ruminatively — at the hat Rob had folded into his epaulette on entering the house, the shiny black toes of his shoes and the knife-edge creases in his trousers.

'I see,' he said. 'In the *salott*, yes?' He led the way into the formal room and waved Rob to a small red sofa, white lace antimacassars placed precisely on its back.

Whilst Rita prepared cold drinks in the kitchen Gwann kept charge of the conversational ball, enquiring after Rob's family and how life was treating him up at the barracks at Mtarfa.

And all the time that he exchanged courtesies with Rob, his eyes flickered back to his daughter, measuring, assessing, looking into her heart until she felt quite clammy with nerves.

Finally, when Rita had returned with a cloth-covered tray and made sure, with careful hospitality, that everybody had a cold drink, Gwann turned an enquiring face to Rob.

'You wish to say something to me?'

'Yes, sir.' This came easily to Rob's lips. Sylvana had heard it often when they met an off-duty officer that Rob knew and he said, 'Evening, sir,' as they passed.

But, from there, Rob seemed stuck, clearing his throat as if searching for the words he wanted. His fair skin reddened across his cheeks and nose.

Gwann waited.

Rob sipped his drink and replaced the glass on the mat Rita had placed on the polished table.

Butterflies fluttered in Sylvana's chest. If Rob didn't say it soon, she'd blurt it out herself! How could her father not know what Rob was trying to ask, anyway? He must have guessed! Why else would Rob ask to see him?

Finally, Rob found his voice.

'Sir, I love your daughter very much. You know that we've been seeing each other for nearly a year now. And we want to get married.'

Silence.

Sylvana dared a glance at her father, whose eyes were fixed on Rob. In the other chair, Rita moved quickly and then subsided. Through the heavy hush, Rob ploughed on.

'I'm not a rich man but, as a staff

8

sergeant, I can afford to support a wife.'

Gwann's face gave away little of his thoughts.

Rob's voice began to steady.

'We'd like to marry here, in Malta, in the church that your family attends.'

The Odd One Out

Gwann shifted his gaze from Rob to Sylvana and then back to Rob. 'Marriage.'

'Yes, sir.'

'A marriage between two people from different countries has many difficulties,' Gwann observed eventually. 'The Army will take you away from Malta, Mr Denton. The Army is good to you. It gives you a job and a place to live.

'But what about Sylvana? Always, she will be the odd one out. A British Army wife but not British.'

'There are wives of all nationalities. Anyway, we'll have each other.' Rob sounded edgy.

'And you are older than she is.'

'Yes, nine years. It makes me steadier than a younger man.'

Gwann's gaze moved to his daughter. 'You've never left Malta before.'

She smiled at the love and concern in his eyes.

'I've been to Sicily twice, on the ferry!'

His eyes twinkled as he inclined his head.

'I forgot. But his next posting will not be a short holiday, it will be for years. It might be to Britain. But it might be to Hong Kong or Gibraltar.'

Her heart was racing. It sounded splendid!

'It's what I want. I love Rob.' She let her chin tilt in the air.

Slowly, Gwann nodded.

'For months I have been able to see this. But I am scared to lose my daughter. All my other children have been content to marry someone who lives on the island.'

So Happy

Rita reached out and touched her husband's hand.

'So many Maltese are leaving Malta to find work. She could marry a Maltese boy and still go off into the world. Maltese are emigrating to Britain, to Australia, America and Canada. Since the war, they have done this.'

Gwann sighed. But then she'd be married to someone who called the same country home.

'Mr Denton, what does your Army say if you get married?' He had never called Rob by his first name.

Rob grinned ruefully.

'My commanding officer says pretty much the same as you, pointing out all the pitfalls. He always gives a darned good pep talk to any of the lads wanting to marry a local girl. He just said — ' He halted.

'He said . . . ?'

Rubbing his nose, Rob grimaced.

'He'd like to think that Sylvana's

parents don't object.'

Sylvana felt her heart plummet and wished Rob wasn't quite so honest. he'd just given her father all he needed to scupper them, as Rob would say. She moved suddenly. She didn't want to make her father angry but her feelings were boiling up.

'I love Rob!' she burst out. 'And I'm twenty-three!'

Gwann nodded.

'And you don't need my permission,' he finished for her. He sighed again and looked at his wife.

Sylvana switched from one to the other, trying to read the messages that seemed, as so often, to pass through the air between her parents. They weren't a demonstrative couple but feelings between them ran deep.

'We don't object,' Gwann said slowly, at last.

'Papa!' Sylvana bounced to her feet, grasping her father's shoulders and planting big kisses on both of his cheeks and his forehead. 'I'm so happy! Oh,

Rob!' She threw her arms around him.

And Rob was laughing down at her, returning her hug. Then he reached past her, extending his hand to his future father-in-law.

'You've made us both very happy, Mr Bonnici.' And to Rita, 'Mrs Bonnici.' And, finally, back to Sylvana. 'Well, Mrs Denton-to-be, we'd better start looking for a ring!'

Sylvana embraced each of her parents in turn, delighted that they smiled and managed wishes of happiness in her marriage, but conscious that they didn't so much approve of her choice as accept it.

Her mother's prosaic voice broke into her thoughts.

'And now we will meet Lino and his family. Do you come with us?'

Sylvana grinned. She might be an unofficially engaged woman but her mother still didn't intend to leave her alone with Rob!

'Thank you, but we're going to Valletta this evening.' It was a precious evening, a landmark to be savoured with the man she loved. She wasn't ready yet to let her big brother Lino tease her about it!

★ ★ ★

Sylvana and Robert had made them late and it was dark now. Rita and Gwann strolled side-by-side along and down Tower Road, the reverse of Sylvana and Rob's journey earlier. A neat couple, neither of them tall but each with their share of dignity.

In Maltese, Rita murmured, 'You gave your permission?' She made it a question.

Gwann gazed up at the stars in the black velvet sky.

'She's twenty-three. Forbidding her from marrying him will do no good and it might do harm. Cause trouble. Cut her off from her family — who she might need, one day. She's young and has a strong head and a full heart. I can't prevent her from marrying him.' They paused at the kerb to allow a grey Morris Minor to turn into a narrow street.

Down the hill they strolled, smiling and calling greetings whenever they met one of the many friends they'd made through living in Sliema all of their lives, until they could see the dark, oily glint of the sea in Sliema Creek at night, the Magic Kiosk and the green-painted tables set around it lit with strings of coloured bulbs.

Lino and Tereza waited beneath the trees, sipping soft drinks from tall glasses. As soon as they caught sight of Gwann and Rita they called the children.

'Gordon, Charles! Look, Josie! Here are Nanna and Nannu!'

As three little faces swung towards her, Rita found herself beaming.

'Sorry to be late! We've been talking to Sylvana.' She thanked Gwann as he pulled out a chair for her and she sank down on to it, crossing her sandaled feet neatly at the ankles.

Gwann nodded at his son.

'I see you are Tom Jones again?'

Lino laughed, touching the big collar of his white shirt, open at his neck to show a small gold St Christopher medal.

'I am in fashion!'

Ruffling the hair of Charles and Gordon and pinching the chubby cheek of brown-eyed Josie, Gwann took his own seat.

'Have you waited for us to buy ice-cream?'

'Yes! Yes!' the boys called, while little Josie crowed from her pushchair.

Curious

Gwann and Rita settled down to spend a precious hour with the family, joking and exchanging news with their son and daughter-in-law, spoiling the children.

And although Lino gave them a curious look from time to time, as if waiting to be told what it was they'd been talking to their daughter about, it was unlikely that he guessed that they'd just been told Sylvana was getting married.

But across Marsamxett Harbour in the island's fortress city capital, Valletta,

Sylvana and Rob were having trouble talking about anything else! They hopped off the green-bodied, white-roofed bus that had carried them around the moon-lit creeks of Sliema, Msida and Pieta and through the broad streets of Floriana to the circular terminus at the Triton Fountain, and made their way to the Upper Barracca gardens where they took possession of a wooden bench to admire the view over Grand Harbour.

Graceful stone arches that ran across the gardens cast strange shadows on the wide viewing platform. The lights of Cottonera, on the other side of the harbour, reflected on the black water like golden scribbles, and twinkling pinpricks shone from the little boats that crossed busily from side to side.

Letters

'I feel like lemonade!' Sylvana whispered, her hand warm in Rob's.

'We can find a café . . .'

She bubbled with laughter.

'No! I feel as if I'm made of lemonade! Fizzing!'

His laugh was low and quiet in the darkness. His hand squeezed hers.

'It might be more sophisticated to say champagne but I feel exactly the same! And so relieved to have that interview with your dad over. At least he didn't toss me out on my ear!' He sobered. 'He hasn't thrown obstacles in our way but I don't think your parents are very pleased. Do you?'

Sylvana sighed.

'Not really,' she admitted. 'They are worried about me moving around the world with the Army, worried I'll be lonely. No, not lonely . . . ' She hunted for the right words.

'A fish out of water,' Rob supplied.

She hadn't heard that English expression before but it summed up what she meant.

'Yes — a fish out of the water, away from my home, my family, my friends.'

'Do you think you can bear it?' he

murmured. 'I don't want to make you lonely. You've loads of friends here in Malta and you're very close to your family.'

'I will be all right.' But her voice wavered.

His fingers tightened around hers.

'I'll always look after you. You'll be the centre of my world.'

Sylvana's smile was brilliant.

'Then I'll be OK. As long as I have you.'

★   ★   ★

In the following months, Sylvana whirled through a host of firsts. It was so exciting to be engaged! After the most thrilling shopping trip of her life, Rob bought her a ring, gold and emerald, and placed it upon the third finger of her left hand.

'That's for always,' he said.

She met some of Rob's comrades from Mtarfa in the north of the island where the barracks, along with the military hospital, sat on the skyline with a clear view across to the historic and silent city of Mdina.

And she invested a lot of time and care in the choosing of a pattern and a fabric like white pearl for her wedding dress, talking over every detail with her mother and the local dressmaker, Maria, who, handily, was her godmother.

'You will be the most beautiful bride that Stella Maris Church has ever seen!' Maria declared. And every morning when Sylvana heard the beautiful deep toll of the church bell her stomach would skip and her heart would beat up into her throat. In a few short months, she and Rob would be standing under the painted dome before the priest to make their vows.

She made a wedding list of portable items like plates and saucepans because Rob had told her that he'd put his name down for a married quarter and, if he got one, it would come furnished. If not, they'd have to rent privately, but that would come furnished, too. Army people didn't seem to buy furniture and she could see it would be expensive to transport to the next posting.

She really hoped that they'd get a married quarter. She knew where there were some in Tigne Barracks, beside Sliema, on Tigne Point, and they looked lovely, bright places with children playing outside in the sun and a school nearby with the railings painted a cheerful blue. And she'd like to have Army wives in homes either side of hers. It would make her feel as if she was part of everything. Their quarter would be up at Mtarfa but she supposed it would look much the same — all the barracks had been built in similar style, long buildings of the local golden stone with arches running across the front.

She learned to assess the rank of off-duty soldiers in civvies simply by whether they stopped and joked with Rob, said, 'Evening, staff sergeant!' to him or he said, 'Evening, sir!' to them.

And when one of Rob's mates said, 'So you're the future Mrs Denton!' her cheeks glowed. But if they added, 'We'll be at the church to see he makes an honest woman of you!' her smile would slide straight off.

They used that phrase a lot, the British servicemen, and she felt it wasn't a nice saying. Asking Rob for an explanation hadn't exactly reassured her and she hoped none of them said it in front of Papa!

She was glad that they didn't socialise much with the rowdiest of the soldiers, and they'd soon be hopping up into a *karrozzin*, one of the domed horse-drawn carriages that the soldiers called a '*gharri*', a word they seemed to have brought with them from India.

Another first was that Sylvana received letters from Rob's family in Yorkshire, England! A positive stream of them came from Rob's little sister, Denise, who, a full eighteen years younger than him, at fourteen seemed to have a bad case of hero worship for Rob and fully prepared to extend it to Sylvana. Denise's school photo showed a rosy blonde girl with freckles and a deep fringe beaming at the camera. Her letters, full of warmth, cheered Sylvana with their ingenuous enthusiasm.

I want to get to know you, if you're going to marry our Robbie, because I've never had a sister-in-law before! she wrote and, before long, she was confiding all her schoolgirl tragedies.

The letter from Rob's mum Ida Denton, was more laboured and, it had to be said, less enthusiastic.

We hope you understand that we can't be at the wedding, Ida wrote. *I never thought I'd miss our Robert's wedding day but we just can't afford the airfare. And that's before we even begin to think about putting up in a hotel.*

Sylvana thought Rob would be dismayed that his parents wouldn't attend the big day but Rob merely shrugged.

'I knew they couldn't come out here, darling. We'll see them as soon as we can get home on leave.'

Floating on a cloud of love Sylvana was quite prepared to take his word for it. Whenever Rob called her 'darling' she was likely to forget what they been talking about!

Exotic

Rob liked to get away from Mtarfa and they spent much of their time together walking around the road that flowed around the bastions of Valletta, the stone ramparts soaring up to the citadel on one side and down to the sea on the other, so that they could talk quietly about the life they were going to begin together before making for a café when they'd worked up a thirst.

'I suppose whichever country we get married in, one family will be disappointed,' Sylvana mused.

His blue eyes settled on her.

''Fraid so. I expect Mum and Dad'll have a party for my lot when we're in the UK.'

To Sylvana's surprise, it was her parents who were disturbed when Sylvana showed them her future mother-in-law's letter. Gwann frowned.

'A hotel is expensive! You must tell them that they are welcome to stay here! In Freddie and Lino's old room.'

Rob grinned.

'That's really generous of you, Mr Bonnici. And I've offered to help them with the air fare but, to be honest, neither of them has any intention of setting foot on an aeroplane!'

So long as Rob could face the absence of his parents Sylvana was quite happy to prepare for an unremitting sea of khaki on the groom's side of the church, but Gwann and Rita quite obviously felt very sorry for both Rob and his parents, as Sylvana discovered when Gwann sat her down for a serious talk.

'Marrying a man from a different country will always cause problems like this. Always you will have to make choices. Where will your children be born? What if the first is born here and the next in England?'

Sylvana gave him a reassuring hug.

'It won't matter! That's what Army children are like! You hear them boasting about where they were born and where they have lived — the more exotic, the better.'

What she didn't tell him was that there was a strong rumour already about where the squadron would go next — there seemed a good chance that her first child would be born in Germany. And she was well aware her father wouldn't want to know that she was really looking forward to Rob being posted away from Malta.

'My parents would be horrified,' she confided, as they sat in a pavement café with the sea frothing on the rocky foreshore across the road. 'I love them dearly but Sliema is a small place and Malta is a small country. My mother and my father are both from big families and wherever I go there are eyes to watch me!'

Rob pulled a face.

'That's Malta! Everybody knows everybody and everybody owns a boat!' He nodded at the dozens of little boats moored out in the creek. His face grew serious. 'It really will be a different life for you when I'm posted away from here. We might be hours from the sea.'

'I know, I know!' she cried. 'It will be an adventure!'

To live where no-one would much worry about watching over her, even though Sylvana was a well-behaved young woman, certainly held appeal, as she dreamed of a golden life of globetrotting with Rob.

She felt sorry for Rob's parents not relishing the idea of air travel because it was a long-held dream for her to step into a big white airliner, strap herself in and wait to be brought cups of tea by the stewardess, a lifestyle she'd so far only seen in films at the Alhambra on the corner of the Strand.

'Do you think the squadron will go to Germany?'

Rob lifted his eyebrows.

'It might. We telecomm lads get sent all over, though, so I wouldn't rely on it. A lot depends on what courses you've been on.'

Sylvana didn't want to see her daydream evaporate so readily.

'But you might go?' She dimpled. 'In fact . . . we might!'

He caught her hand.

'As long as you turn up at that church in a fortnight!'

She laughed up at him, brown eyes glowing.

'I will if you will! Oh, Rob! Won't it be wonderful? Not long to wait now. I wish we had got a married quarter, though. I don't want to start married life living in my parents' home!'

He pulled a face.

'I don't fancy that, either. If a quarter hasn't come through by the time we return from our honeymoon on Gozo, we'll just find somewhere to rent until it does.'

Bombshell

'Only a few days!' Sylvana whirled around her bedroom, long hair flying from the beaded elastic circlet that caught it up at the top of her head, getting in the way of her big sister, Martina, who had elected to let her husband take their children to watch a football match at the Empire Stadium in Gzira whilst she helped Sylvana with the hundred and one jobs that awaited a young woman whose wedding was on Saturday.

The job in hand was to press and pack up the tablecloths and pillow-cases that Sylvana had collected for her 'bottom drawer', but Sylvana's attention was more on the future than on filling her smart, new red vinyl-covered case.

'Sylvana!' Martina scolded, snatching up the electric iron before Sylvana could knock it off the ironing-board. 'Calm down!'

Instead, Sylvana threw her arms around her sister and kissed her cheek.

'What colour are you wearing to the wedding?'

Martina pretended to tut.

'I've already told you all about my outfit!'

'Tell me again!'

'I have a lemon paisley sleeveless dress with a high neck and white sleeves and a lemon bolero with white piping. And silver sandals that — '

'Sylvana!' Gwann's voice echoed sharply up the stairwell. 'Sylvana! Robert is here. Please come down.'

Sylvana stared at Martina and her heart gave a thump.

'Rob isn't due to call for me tonight! I wonder what — ' Her heart gave an even bigger thump and her eyes grew round as she clutched her sister's arms. 'Perhaps we've been given a quarter! Martina, do you think that could be?'

Prosaically, Martina released herself and picked up a white pillow-case with blue scalloped edging.

'How would I know what goes on in the British Army? Why not go and find out?'

Abandoning her sister to the linen, Sylvana ran all the way down the narrow, tiled staircase and into the *salott*.

Rob turned the instant she flew in. As usual, he looked out of place in uniform against the rich wooden furniture and bits of lace with which Rita liked to decorate her best room.

'Rob! Do you have news?' Sylvana burst out.

And then she saw her father, standing a little apart, his face set.

She hesitated, feeling the beaming smile slide from her face at her father's expression.

'Hello, love.' Rob's smile was a pale imitation of his usual broad grin. He glanced at Gwann, who gazed steadily back, hovering protectively.

'Robert tells me he has something you must talk about,' he said.

Heart suddenly racing, Sylvana's eyes fastened on her fiancé.

'What is it?'

Stepping closer, Rob took her hands. 'I've got something to tell you, yes.'

Sylvana felt her throat dry. Suddenly,

31

she realised that Rob's grave expression didn't augur good news.

His fingers were warm upon hers.

'I'm being sent to a unit in Singapore. Some bloke's been taken ill and I have to replace him pretty much straight away.'

She searched his face.

'Will we get a married quarter there?'

Rob looked unhappy.

'I'm afraid not. It's a single posting.'

Alarm flickered through Sylvana.

'What does that mean?'

Gently, and despite Gwann's glower, Rob took her in his arms.

'It means I have to go out there as if I'm a single man. There's no place for my wife. It's for about eleven months, that's when the regiment I'll be attached to moves on.'

Hot tears burned suddenly in Sylvana's eyes, spilling over to slide down her cheeks.

'Eleven months! And I'm to stay here? Without you? But what if the other man gets better?'

Rob pulled a face.

'It'll be a long time before that happens, apparently. I'm so sorry, darling.'

'Can't someone else go?'

'Specialist knowledge,' he said briefly.

'And can you refuse?' She knew what his reply would be, even as he made it. She'd heard it from him before.

'No. It's what I signed up for.'

Her voice was no more than a thread and cold sweat was gathering at the base of her neck.

'When? When do you go?'

He kissed her temple, whispering into her hair.

'Wednesday.'

For a moment the room swam about her.

'Not Wednesday! We marry on Saturday!'

'We can have about two days of our honeymoon then I'll have to report back to camp. I've got RAF transport to Lynham, then on to Changi.'

Suddenly, Gwann was beside Sylvana, his voice compassionate, yet with an edge of anger.

'The wedding will be postponed, Sylvana, of course. You will have plenty of time to . . . consider, whilst Robert is in Singapore.' His dark eyes flicked accusingly to Rob, showing anger that his daughter was hurt and that Rob was the cause of it.

Rob flushed.

'I'm sorry, Mr Bonnici. If I could change things, I would. I didn't want this to happen. But I've got my orders and I've seen my squadron commander. I have to do as the Army says. It's what I signed up for,' he repeated.

Throwing up his hands, Gwann returned to a frozen Sylvana.

'It is what I warned you. The Army says this, the Army says that, and your life is changed!'

Rob gathered Sylvana closer, a statue in his arms.

'My squadron commander asked if I was going to postpone the wedding, too.' His face fell into lines of misery. 'It seems as if everybody thinks it's the right thing to do.'

'Anything else would be madness,' Gwann agreed.

Sylvana was in a spin. The beautiful bedclothes that Martina was ironing upstairs whirled through her mind, the church, the altar boys, the hymns she'd chosen and the elegant ivory wedding invitations that had been accepted with such lovely notes from her family and friends.

Mrs Sammut was shutting the shop to come to the wedding; old school-friends had dipped into their modest wages to make a collection and buy her and Rob a beautiful canteen of cutlery.

Last week she'd even gone with Rob to see two apartments, as their hopes for a married quarter had sunk. And they had seen apartments where she would have been quite content to begin her married life, their first home, her first foray into adulthood and independence. Small but sufficient. She could use her own beautiful bedlinen and unpack all their bright new wedding presents.

Their first home.

She saw it all fading away. Saw the honeymoon clothes being unpacked and the linens returned forlornly to their bottom drawer.

Instinctively, she realised that as Rob's fiancée she would always be this easy to sweep aside. But as his wife . . .

'No!' she declared, letting her arms tighten around him. 'We'll get married. I will wait here for you until the Army lets us be together. We'll have the wedding and the honeymoon and I'll wait here, working at the pharmacy as usual, until you come back for me.'

'But . . . ' Gwann burst out.

She turned to her father, battling to squeeze back her tears and steady her voice.

'I know you're concerned for me. But if I postpone the wedding then I will have failed my first test as an Army wife the first time Rob has to do his duty. I have to take the bad with the good. It's what I'm signing up for! We have time to get married before Rob goes away.

And that's what we're going to do!'
 'Good girl!' Rob breathed
 She managed a watery smile
 'I'll be here. Waiting.'

Excitement

The sands of their time together ran out all too quickly.

Sylvana had completed her wedding preparations with a smile on her face that felt as if it were made of wax. The scheduled events ticked past. The hairdresser arrived to dress her hair in an extravagant bouffant 'do' over which her headdress and veil would sit, as white as her thick, lustrous hair was dark. Martina and Rita painted her nails opal pink and helped her into her narrow satin dress with its square neckline and little train. Her breakfast she could hardly touch for excitement.

Walking into church on Gwann's arm, she passed suits, bright dresses and lace fans on her right and a block of khaki on her left as the solemn music filled the air. The service: kind Father Gorg's voice rolling out over the congregation, comforting in its familiarity as it spoke the words that would tie her to Rob for ever.

And Rob.

Quiet and reassuring, love glowing from his blue eyes when he winked at her as Father Gorg turned away, making her want to giggle. His voice firm as he gave his vows but his fingers trembling very slightly as he struggled to get the plain gold band on to her finger.

At that moment, the tall, self-possessed soldier became her husband.

The rest of the day passed in a blur and the two days in their little hotel on Gozo seemed to go faster, and it seemed only minutes until they were leaving Gozo's natural harbour, Mgarr, on the ferry across the narrow band of water to Cirkewwa.

Back to chilly reality, where Rob would have transport ready to whisk him back into the arms of the Army that was waiting to fly him away from Malta. And Gwann and Rita would pick up Sylvana in Gwann's little black Ford Prefect and take her home.

Her parents' home. Her old room. The room where she'd always lived, where she would slip back into the life she had been leading but for the golden ring upon her finger. A married woman without husband or home.

Her name would be Sylvana Denton — and she would make certain everybody used it! — but Rob Denton would be far away.

★ ★ ★

On the short crossing between the islands they stood together at the starboard rail, watching the race of white-tipped waves, shoulders touching.

Sylvana had tied a blue headscarf around her hair to prevent the sea breeze teasing the tendrils free. It went well with her blue patterned dress that she'd kept to wear until this last precious day of their honeymoon because it was Rob's favourite and she wanted him to remember her looking her best.

Around her neck was a necklace he'd bought her of large silver beads that popped together and silver gypsy rings in her ears.

She wanted to leave him a memory that was colourful and bright and had pasted a determined smile on her lips on rising that morning, a smile that didn't feel part of her but which she was determined to keep in place.

Even if her heart was like a lump of grey lead.

'How often will you write?'

'Lots,' he said, pressing his shoulder still harder against hers. 'You?'

'Every day.' Her smile was making her face ache almost as much as her heart.

'I'll miss you.'

'And you'll let me know when they give you the next posting?'

'Instantly. It won't be another single posting, they wouldn't do that.'

'I hope not!' Her laugh sounded almost like a sob. 'Or you'll have to go absent without leave!'

He stroked her forearm where it lay golden along the white rail.

'They'd pick me up in no time — they'd know I'd be wherever you are.'

'Then I would have to hide you very, very well.'

'Eleven months. Eleven months and we'll be back together.'

'Eleven months,' she repeated, shivering, even though the sun was bright and strong. 'I wish it didn't sound so long. But I'll be waiting for you.'

'It won't seem such a huge chunk of our life together when we look back on it.' He grinned suddenly. 'Not much happens in eleven months!'

2

1969

Sylvana's heart was thumping as she waited at Luqa airport, hardly aware of the white tiled floor and high ceilings or of other passengers emerging with their luggage trolleys, creased and tired after long flights to the island of Malta.

All her attention was focused on waiting for one face. So fiercely did she will him to appear that she'd even stopped wondering whether her new red baby-doll dress and white sandals had been the right choice or how long it would take to get back home to her parents' house.

Then . . . there! Finally! A tall figure, almost unfamiliar out of uniform and in 'civvies', was striding along with a khaki cardboard suitcase in his hand and a cylindrical kitbag on his shoulder.

'Rob!'

Her voice emerged hoarsely but, instantly, Rob swung her way.

'Sylvana!' Case and kitbag abandoned, Rob strode across the tiles, his face one enormous beaming smile. Like magnets, Sylvana's hands flew into his and for several moments the bustle of the airport, other people, other voices, faded as brown eyes gazed into blue.

His fingers gripped hers so tightly that it hurt and yet Sylvana still had trouble believing that he was real. Her gaze searched his face, reassuring herself that it was still as full of love for her as ever. As he tried to pull her closer, breathlessly she clung to decorum.

'There's a taxi waiting. We need to go home.'

'Oh, good grief, yes.' Rob released her hands, laughing. 'Let's go!'

Gwann, Sylvana's father, had offered to drive her to and from the airport but Sylvana had opted for the anonymity of a taxi, reluctant to share these first minutes with anyone. She had rarely ridden in a taxi before but today was something special.

And once his bags were stowed and the taxi had set off, Rob pulled Sylvana into his arms and kissed her breathless. She certainly wouldn't have liked her father sitting in the front of the car for that.

Now, all she could think about was the warmth of his arms around her, the wonderful reality of knowing that the weary months had passed. The eleven months he'd been in Singapore had been busier than she'd anticipated but, still, she had missed him with a bone-deep ache.

She was almost giddy by the time she had the opportunity to speak.

'My parents are going out for the rest of the day. But they're overjoyed that you've been posted back to Malta.'

His eyes glowed down into hers.

'It almost never happens. But now that the British are leaving the island the Army wants me here because I've got local knowledge of the systems. It might be for as long as a year!'

44

Sylvana sighed rapturously.

'And there will be a married quarter for us!'

Rob laughed.

'As people are leaving and not being replaced, I should think we'll be able to have our pick of them! It'll be a very funny barracks. But that's Army life for you — you never know what's going to happen next.'

Finally, the dusty black taxi drew up outside the house of Sylvana's parents and Rob paid the driver whilst Sylvana fidgeted impatiently. She could hardly wait to take Rob indoors.

Several neighbours were in the street, casting looks at Rob that were either friendly, shy or frankly curious, but Sylvana prayed that none would detain them. Tomorrow she would be sociable — today she had something far more pressing to do.

'Come on!' She bustled Rob in through the front door to where her parents waited in the hall, Rita tidying her already tidy hair in the mirror.

'Robert!' First Gwann and then Rita shook hands with Rob, and Rita kissed Sylvana on each cheek.

'In the *sallot*,' she whispered. 'We have made arrangements for a lovely day out. See you later!'

The front door clicked closed and, left alone with her husband in the cool quiet of the stone building, Sylvana thought she would burst with emotion. Too choked to speak, she took an equally silent Rob by the hand and led him into the *sallot*, where, along with the sofa and the polished table, stood a brand-new piece of furniture — a small wooden crib.

Tucked under the cotton blanket slept a baby, brown curls clustered around her head, tiny lips pursed as if dreaming of her bottle. Downy eyelashes fluttered on soft cheeks.

Rob sucked in an unsteady breath.

Gently, Sylvana scooped up the precious infant and turned to face her husband.

'Here she is,' she whispered. 'Elena Melita Denton.' Fresh tears started, although her heart was bursting with happiness. 'Here is your daughter.'

Family Home

It took only an instant for Rob to fall in love. He would remember this moment for the rest of his life. Photographs of Elena, who had been born just a couple of months ago, hadn't touched him like this. The reality was so much more poignant and beautiful.

As if in a dream, he dropped on to the sofa and held out his arms. Sylvana gave to him the slight weight of his daughter and, gently, he drew the little bundle close against his heart. One delicate baby hand, lying outside the white lacy wrapper, opened suddenly into a tiny star.

Dimly, he was aware of Sylvana sinking down beside him as he gazed and gazed at his daughter as if he'd never be able to tear his eyes away. As if he could sit in this silent room and hold her safe for the rest of his life.

His mind flew to the night that he'd asked Gwann for permission to marry Sylvana and how Gwann hadn't tried to disguise his misgivings and concerns about his daughter's happiness. And, suddenly, Rob understood! The mantle of fatherhood settled on his shoulders, a deep, unconditional love and fearsome protectiveness that would remain with him for as long as he drew breath.

As he watched, Elena stretched and uncurled in his arms and opened her eyes, drowsily. Her eyes were the same deep brown as Sylvana's.

'Hello!' Rob whispered. 'Elena Melita, I'm your daddy. I think I must be the happiest daddy in the world. And to think that when I left I said to your mother, 'Not much can happen in eleven months!' But, look! A whole new person has arrived!'

He turned to Sylvana.

'I'm the luckiest man alive.' Cautiously, he freed an arm to slide it around his wife. 'I think she must be the most beautiful baby ever born.'

For Sylvana, the next few weeks were unbelievably exciting as, in quick succession, she found herself the proud joint possessor of a car, a pet and a married quarter at Mtarfa Barracks.

The car was a cream-coloured 1960 Mercedes that Rob was able to buy quite reasonably from one of the shoal of departing servicemen. Now that new Forces personnel were not materialising, there was a glut of cars to dispose of and the Mercedes had lived an eventful life, judging by the scrapes and dents that ornamented its body and the cracks in the red leather interior. But, when Rob turned up in the car for the first time, a birdcage on the back seat and its stand pushed rakishly through an open window, Sylvana's excitement turned to amazement.

'What is this?'

'They threw the budgie in when I bought the car.' Rob's face creased with his ready smile. 'His name's Joey and if I hadn't taken him I don't know what might have happened, British quarantine laws being as strict as they are. C'mon, pass me that carry cot and we'll take Elena to see her new home!'

Sylvana tutted.

'We can't leave a bird in the car all afternoon. The sun is hot! We'll have to carry him up to my room.'

Joey was a fine bird with a body as blue as the Maltese sky and a cloud-white head. Flitting from perch to perch, he flicked up the seed and water that had upset on the journey and Sylvana carried him indoors gingerly.

'What's that?' Rita, her lilac dress neatly covered by a floral apron, was at the kitchen door as if attuned to anything less than spotless that entered her domain.

Sylvana halted guiltily.

'Rob has got us a bird.' She sighed. 'He's eager to make a family home.'

Rita raised her eyebrows.

'Well, don't take it upstairs! Put the bird in the shade of the *bitha* where the mess does not matter.'

Grateful that she didn't have to spend time soothing her houseproud mother, Sylvana abandoned the cage gladly in the courtyard behind the house and raced back outside to where Rob was cooing at Elena in her navy carry cot.

'Come on,' he cried, as if the delay was nothing to do with him. 'Let's get off to see our new place!'

Twenty minutes later they were bowling towards a barracks on the highest point of Malta, the island laid out in all directions about them, villages punctuated by splendid churches, brown and green farmland built up in terraces to prevent soil erosion when the occasionally ferocious rains came.

The Merecedes purred past the guardhouse and past a red-and-white barrier that seemed to be permanently in the 'up' position. From the tall, narrow clock tower to the khaki of the Army trucks, Sylvana could scarcely take everything in. Except that the barracks was beginning to look very empty.

'We'll Manage'

The married quarters were long, low two-storey buildings of flat roofs and rows of arches, basking golden in the sunshine. The quarters that were no longer in use now the Army had begun its withdrawal from the island were closed up tightly. They stood, silently, in rows.

Sylvana almost shivered.

The barracks on the top of the hill, so much a feature of Malta for so long, used to be alive with soldiers beating the ground with their big black boots, their families busy about their lives, the courtyards between the married quarters brisk with lines of washing drying in the sun and prams and playpens in the shade, the older children arguing over the rules of hopscotch or risking their necks on brightly coloured bikes or clattering metal roller-skates. But now it seemed as if weeds were already growing in the cracks in the yards.

'It is quiet,' she ventured.

Rob nodded.

'A lot of the lads have gone home since I left.' But then he smiled. 'At least the Army leaving means that I've got a bonus few months on the island.'

They drew up before one of the long buildings where the windows were thrown open to catch the breeze and the yards were still full of life.

'Do you know how long you — we — will be here for? Or where you'll be posted next?'

Rob laughed at Sylvana's eagerness.

'No and no! Nobody has told me anything beyond I'm to stay here for as long as I'm needed and that I'll go when I'm needed somewhere else.' He grinned. 'But I must be due a home posting soon!'

He threw open his car door.

'C'mon, Mrs Denton. Let's get this home sorted out before we begin to worry about the next!'

Each building was arranged rather like a terrace of flat-topped houses but the staircases to the upper storey gave away that they were, in fact, flats. A stone balustrade safely fenced in the walkway behind the arches on the upper part of the building and a matching balustrade edged the roof.

It didn't take Rob long to identify the door to number 5, Harlech Road, painted pale blue like all the others.

'This is it!' he said. And, with a grin, he turned the key and led Sylvana into the cool depths.

The curtains were closed against the sun, but Rob threw them back in every room. And it didn't take long to view the ground-floor flat with its two bedrooms, a kitchen big enough to take a table, a lounge and a bathroom with a shower attachment over the bath. Tiled floors were cool in the relentless heat and all the walls were painted white. Pale grey ceiling fans hung motionless in every room.

Their voices echoed emptily, making Sylvana feel as if she ought to whisper.

'It's beautiful!' she breathed.

'Smashing,' Rob agreed. 'A lot better than we'd have got when the Army was at full strength. Elena can have her own bedroom. If the flat was any bigger Joey could have his own room, too!'

She giggled.

'He must live in the *sallot*. No, the lounge,' she corrected herself.

Rob dropped a kiss on her upturned face.

'So. Do you want the flat?'

Sylvana nodded.

'Oh, yes! It will be wonderful, Rob. I want us to be a real family, on our own! With my own kitchen and our own bathroom.' She broke away to gaze with satisfaction at the black-and-white bathroom with the shiny chrome taps. The cistern and the hot water geyser looked a little old-fashioned and well worn but she knew she'd get used to them. As she would the big pot sink in the kitchen.

'Then I'd better go and sign on the dotted line . . . if you're certain that you don't want to stay at your parents' house?' he teased. 'No? We could salt a lot of my pay away, that way.'

Sylvana felt her smile fade. She'd thought

she would try to hang on to her job when Rob went to Singapore. Although a married woman's role was generally seen as being in the home, she had had no home! And her husband had been far away. But, of course, motherhood had changed everything and it was a long time since she'd received a brown wages envelope at the end of the week.

'Can we afford to live here and to have a car?' she asked seriously. 'Tell me if we can't. We could find somewhere cheaper or . . .'

But Rob just threw back his head and roared his big laugh.

'I was pulling your leg, love! We'll have enough to live on, what with my pay and the Family Allowance. I expect we'll have to watch the pennies a bit, but we'll manage.'

★   ★   ★

Within a fortnight, Sylvana was installed in her first home as a married lady. She had pleasant roads along which to wheel

56

Elena's pram and gaze out at the magnificent views across the valley to the beautiful dome and towers of the cathedral like a coronet on the walled city of Mdina and the spread of villages and farms right across the island.

She had a nice flat. And she had a husband who came home to her each evening with a smile to split his face in two, shouting, 'I'm here, love! How are my two girls?'

Escape!

Brought up to be capable of running a household, Sylvana soon settled into a routine of making bottles for Elena and meals for herself and Rob, dusting the Army furniture — which, to her surprise, wasn't khaki or made out of canvas but really quite modern, smart and totally civilian — and keeping all their clothes clean and nice.

Rob ironed his own uniform, to her surprise — he called it 'pressing', not ironing — and shone his own boots and buttons. Every day, he'd put on his uniform and drive off in the battered Mercedes, leaving Sylvana to enjoy her new home and take care of her beautiful baby. She wasn't lonely.

Well, not much.

She was bound to feel a little strange, in the middle of Malta but not amongst the Maltese. Visiting her parents in Sliema, or any other travel around the island, she would have to leave until Rob was off duty. There was a good bus service but climbing on board with a baby and a pram — she didn't dare to try. There were local shops and, at the weekend, Rob would drive her to Valletta, where they could climb stone steps into the heart of St James Cavalier, part of the old fortifications, and find there, miraculously, a NAAFI shop that sold almost anything she could want.

She was a bit stuck while Rob was at work because she certainly couldn't walk to see any of her family or friends in Sliema. But in a few months Elena would have grown old enough for a pushchair and Sylvana could take that on the bus, folded up. Until then, when Rob had gone to work, she could turn the wireless on to a Maltese programme, Joey the budgie singing along lustily, and let those sounds keep her company.

She smiled shyly at a few of the other wives whenever she went out to walk the baby in the pram and they all smiled back. She wondered if they would ever get further than that.

It was almost the end of her first week in the barracks when disaster struck. Sylvana was tired. Elena had not slept well the night before, wailing plaintively as Sylvana tried everything she could think of to soothe her. She changed her, fed her, gave her gripe water, rocked her and patted her back. But Elena had been in no mood to be mollified.

By mid-morning, Sylvana was desperate to fill her mind with something other than the sound of crying baby and so she fixed the sunshade carefully to the pram and set out to see whether a long walk would lull Elena to sleep. And, thankfully, it did. Sylvana walked until the sun and her thirst drove her back home. Carefully, she eased the big pram up over the doorstep.

All would have been well if she'd left Elena in the hall, but the hall was small and stuffy and Sylvana decided to see whether she could manoeuvre the big-wheeled pram into the lounge, where the window was open to let in the breeze.

That was when a spoked pram wheel and the leg of the stand of Joey's cage became entangled. Unthinkingly, Sylvana continued to push without realising what had happened until too late — the stand crashed to the tiled floor, cage and all.

At the screech of metal on tile, Elena returned instantly to red-faced screaming and, guiltily, Sylvana scooped the baby up into her consoling arms. It was then that she noticed that the door to Joey's cage had burst open.

'Oh, no!' she breathed. Patting Elena's back as the baby subsided into hiccupping sobs and snuggled into the comfort of her neck, Sylvana's eyes flicked hopefully around the room. They settled upon the open window as she sighed.

It was several minutes before she felt that Elena was again sleeping soundly enough to be laid back in her pram. Straight away, she crossed to the window and looked out into the area between her building and the next.

The yard, so busy with children playing, was a little intimidating. Sylvana hung her washing out there, of course, but then she came straight in again. She hadn't yet felt comfortable with leaving her French doors open from the lounge, as many of the women did, but came and went through the front door, on the other side of the flat. But now, casting an anxious look back at Elena, she pushed hard at the metal handle so that the door gave too suddenly and she almost fell through it, coming up short when she realised somebody was walking past.

'*Scusi*,' she gasped.

The woman, her plentiful fair hair held off her face, did a smart side-step.

'Whoops-a-daisy, ducks! No harm done.'
And then, with a keen look at Sylvana's
face, she asked, 'You all right?'

Sylvana glanced around.

'I have lost my budgie bird. He flew away.'

She began on a tangled account of how
Joey had escaped his cage. Unconsciously,
she pressed her palm to her head, which
was thumping from anxiety and lack of
sleep.

'Poor thing,' the woman said comfortably. 'Tell you what, why not put the
cage on the veranda, here, with some
nice food in it? Ten-to-one he'll hop
back in if you leave the door open.'

Sylvana was grateful for such calm
good sense.

'Yes! I'll put some lettuce inside! He
loves lettuce.' She hesitated. 'But first I
will put my daughter in the bedroom,
so she does not wake up.'

When she'd wheeled Elena gently into
their room and parked her beside the
neatly made double bed, Sylvana plucked
some crisp lettuce from the fridge and
carried the cage out into the shade. The

woman was still hovering nearby.

'OK, ducks?' she called. 'I'm Pauline, by the way.'

'Sylvana.' She hovered for a moment once the cage was in place, but it was obvious that Joey wouldn't come back whilst she stood guard, so with another shy smile in Pauline's direction, she stepped back into the flat with a sigh.

A Good Day

About thirty seconds later she shot back out again, clattering the French door wide open.

'He is in the bathroom! The bird is in the bathroom!' she called in the direction of a startled-looking Pauline.

With fumbling fingers she unhooked the cage and scrambled her way back through the doors. Gently, she crept through the bathroom door, hoping Joey wouldn't make a dash for it. But Joey, perched on the white-tiled window-sill, was unconcernedly preening under one wing. He stopped to cock his head at her. More in hope than expectation, Sylvana slowly brought the open door of the cage up level with him and, after a pause for thought, Joey hopped along the door as if it were a little drawbridge, and on to the perch closest to the lettuce.

With a sigh of relief, Sylvana fastened the cage.

In the lounge, the doors still stood ajar and Sylvana could see Pauline laughing with another woman, just outside the arches. Hesitantly, she stepped outside and displayed the cage.

'I have him! He is home.'

Pauline grinned, strolling over to admire Joey as Sylvana hooked cage and stand back together.

'That's a good job! This is Reenie.'

Reenie had sandy hair that she wore tucked behind her ears.

'Hello!' She seemed as friendly as Pauline.

Pauline paused to call up the yard to a child getting too wild with his football before turning back.

'Me and Reenie are about to have a cuppa char in the shade, on the veranda, ducks, before we have to get the kids' lunch. Want one?'

Sylvana knew what a cuppa was. It meant a cup of tea. Suddenly, to sit in the shade and share a few minutes with these ladies sounded wonderful — a bright spot in an otherwise difficult day.

'I would like that. But my baby is asleep.'

'That's all right, ducks. We'll sit here, just outside your door, so you'll hear if she cries. You set some chairs out and I'll put the kettle on. OK?'

The twenty minutes spent sitting on a kitchen chair drinking hot tea and learning a little about Pauline and Reenie, whilst children played noisily in the yard, was an oasis of calm and undemanding company for Sylvana. She got up to tackle the rest of her day feeling that all the anxiety of the night and morning had rolled off her shoulders.

And when Rob came home, asking about her day, she didn't tell him about the grizzly baby or the escaping budgie.

Instead she said, 'It was a good day. I had a cuppa char!'

* * *

Gwann felt strange, driving his Ford Prefect carefully through the valley to where the immense David Bruce Military Hospital fronted the barracks that waited majestically on the crest of the ridge, close to the tall, thin clock tower that could be seen for miles around.

As he turned in at the gate he reflected that, in the restaurant, he was much more used to the Army coming to him, as it were, in the form of off-duty soldiers in 'civvies' spending their money on *timpana* or, very often, something from the more English section of the menu.

The restaurant was very quiet now. The government was trying hard to build up the tourist industry in Malta but he certainly hadn't seen tourists in numbers that would replace the soldiers, sailors and airmen who had eaten his carefully prepared food for so many years.

Rita, very neat and correct in a cream summer dress and new beads, her hair brushed into the customary pleat behind her head, consulted the sketch that their British son-in-law had made for them.

'We follow the road to the left and find the second set of buildings. Do you think it will matter where we park?'

Gwann glanced about him.

'There seems to be plenty of space.'

Rita surveyed the rows of shuttered buildings. A netball post and net still stood to attention at the end of a fenced yard and it was even possible to read where a naughty child had scribbled *I love the Beatles* on a playground wall. Her heart sank.

'Do you think that Sylvana is really happy here? It's so . . . lonely.'

Having wondered the same, Gwann responded gruffly as he drove the car along the dusty road where oleanders flowered each side, white and pink, their sharp scent carried into the car on the warm breeze.

'It's better, here, look. There are people.'

Sure enough, rounding the curve had brought them to where children were playing with a football against the wall — a boy obligingly trapped the black-and-white ball with his foot until Gwann had driven past. A few cars were parked alongside the buildings and adults chatted across the *loggias*. He knew from Sylvana's first visit home last weekend that the British called the *loggias* verandas.

Locating Rob's battle-scarred cream Mercedes, he parked neatly behind it. Then all they had to do was find Sylvana's flat.

Their Daughter's Home

A cheerful woman with her fair hair pushed back by a broad plastic hair band and stretch slacks that fastened beneath her bare feet shielded her eyes against the sun to gaze at them.

'Hello? You lost?'

Turning politely, Gwann said, 'We

are visiting Flat Five.'

'They're at the other side, love. Through the gate and turn right into the yard.'

Trying not to look as out of place as he felt, Gwann led Rita through the gate and almost into a chain of screaming children, holding hands as they raced along and all, apparently, in pursuit of one lone girl with pigtails. The chain dissolved and reformed smoothly the other side of Rita and Gwann and screamed off up the long yard.

And, suddenly, they could see Sylvana, perched on a step with her bare legs and feet emerging from beneath a navy dress polka-dotted in white, Elena in her arms.

'Mama! Papa!' Sylvana beamed in welcome. 'Rob! Mama and Papa are here!'

Rob appeared, spruce in light trousers with shirt and tie, and Gwann was pleased Rita had wanted him to put on a tie, too. Rob and Sylvana both looked smart. Especially now that Sylvana had pushed her feet into sandals and tugged her dress down a bit. He would never get used to the young women in mini skirts! Or bare legs! Rita was always decorously clad in a skirt to her knees and nylons.

But he was determined not to be a disapproving papa on his first visit to his newly married daughter's home. Sylvana looked so happy as she kissed their cheeks awkwardly over the baby. Rob beamed as he welcomed them in and Rita gazed around her.

'A lovely home! And so cool! Dinner smells delicious, Sylvana.'

Rita sounded almost stilted, although she was talking to her own daughter. And Gwann knew that Rita, too, was feeling strange.

Sylvana's smile faltered, as if picking up the unease in the air.

'When Elena has finished her bottle, then dinner will be only half an hour. Would you like Rob to get you a sherry?'

Neither Gwann nor Rita bothered much with alcohol but he could see that Sylvana was playing the hostess for all she was worth.

'Thank you!' he said as if he meant it, and watched Rob open the sideboard, where stood a solitary bottle and six new glasses.

Apprehension

And, suddenly, Gwann wanted to smile. The single set of matching glasses illustrated how much this hospitality was a novelty! When their collection was as mismatched as his and Rita's through breakages and replacements, then he would feel that they had a real family home.

'I have to fetch something from the car,' he said.

Rita glanced up.

'Yes, now is a good time.'

Braving the hooting chain of children — only four in the chain now and perhaps a dozen being chased — Gwann fetched the large, heavy parcel. The children were at the other end of the yard but he held his load tightly nonetheless.

Elena had been passed to her nanna for winding by the time he returned and he was able to kiss Sylvana once more and present her with the prettily wrapped box.

'For your new home. With our wishes to be very, very happy.'

Sylvana's eyes grew round.

'Papa! Thank you!' She glanced at her new husband. Then, in a moment, she was ripping the wrapping, reassuring Gwann that, however much a young woman his daughter had become, the child he'd played with such a short time ago still lingered.

'Oh, Mama,' Sylvana breathed, as she lifted several plates from the box. 'You remembered how much I loved these! But they were so expensive! Rob, aren't they beautiful?'

'Aye, they certainly are.' Rob took the plates to free Sylvana to delve further into the box.

Gwann knew there was six of everything in there; he had refused to settle for four when Rita had taken him to the shop in Valletta where Sylvana had long sighed over the ultra-modern dinner service.

Privately, Gwann thought they were

silly plates, made of green glass and each one shaped like a daisy. He would much rather have bought fine white china rimmed in gold and splashed with violets or roses — although geraniums or prickly pear might have been more appropriate to Malta — but Rita had been unmoving. They might be silly plates to Gwann but they were the height of sophistication and fashion to Sylvana.

Now, watching his dear daughter washing the new dinner service at top speed so that they might eat their meal from it this evening, he was content that Rita had been right.

★ ★ ★

'A lovely meal.' Rita sat back after a dessert of figs and ice-cream with her coffee cup filled with hot espresso, strong and sweet, as she liked it. Gradually, the unfamiliarity of her surroundings had worn off and now Rita was enjoying herself. The children playing so energetically outside had gone home to their beds when the quick darkness had fallen. Rob referred to the children as 'barracks brats', but that seemed a bit rude to Rita, even if he said it with affection.

Gwann moved on to the subject of Rob's new posting.

'So you will be here for a year?'

Rob shrugged.

'I don't know that yet. I'm here until I get posted somewhere else.'

'Will it be to the UK?'

Rob shrugged again.

'I don't know. I do hope to have a home posting.' He smiled at Sylvana. 'I know that that's what my missus would like and it's what I'd expect. But nothing's ever settled in the Army, until the posting's confirmed.'

Rita felt her tummy tighten with apprehension at the direction the conversation was taking.

'Well,' Gwann said slowly, 'I think that we will be going to the UK, too.'

Rob's eyebrows lifted.

Sylvana stared.

'How will that be?' She laughed

uncertainly. 'You are taking a holiday?'

Rita put down her cup and saucer and clenched her hands. Every time she thought of their plans her stomach did a somersault, even though she saw the need for change.

'Not a holiday, no.'

'There's no business for the restaurant with most of the British gone,' Gwann said. 'Soon I think that jobs must begin to go. Already, Mr Zammit, the boss, he has talked about this. We must do something.'

His gaze flickered to Rita for a moment before returning to his daughter.

'So your brother, Lino, Tereza, your mother, me, we will lease a restaurant in Southampton and run it as a family concern. There is room to live above.'

The silence was deafening. Sylvana fumbled her coffee cup down on to the wooden coffee table.

'But that means you'll be living in England before I will!'

3

January 1971

Yorkshire, England — but it might as well have been the North Pole, so far as Sylvana was concerned. A horrible, frozen rain that Rob called 'sleet' flung itself in her face and down the collar of a coat that had been fine for a Maltese January but was no defence against the raw wind funnelling along the station platform.

She clamped her teeth together to prevent them from chattering as she hugged a shawl around a wriggling Elena and scrunched up her fast-stiffening toes in her shoes, waiting for Rob to retrieve the pushchair and suitcases from the guard's van.

Even Rob, Yorkshire born and bred, looked as if he was feeling the cold after three years in Malta and Singapore. His face was pinched with weariness, too. It felt as if they'd been travelling for ever and neither of them had slept on the plane or the train because Elena had cried or crawled or crowed but was never quiet or still; the journey had been long and she hadn't liked the food. Sylvana hadn't been that keen on it herself. In fact, although she'd longed to fly for as long as she could remember, the plane had been nothing but a disappointment.

Heart beating with anticipation, she'd glided across the tarmac and up the aircraft steps, but once on board she'd found the plane rather like a bus, with the seats too close together and passengers trying to arrange their bags around their feet.

'Down!' Elena urged now, squirming.

Sylvana held her tightly.

'Not yet, *bambina*. It is dangerous.' The gusty platform was no place for a two-year-old and Sylvana was convinced that her daughter would freeze if allowed out of the shawl.

'Dad-dee!' Elena stopped wriggling to point excitedly over Sylvana's shoulder, eyes dark and shiny as buttons.

Sylvana turned.

'Yes, Daddy has the suitcases.'

But the suitcases were abandoned on the platform, the navy pushchair, still folded, between them.

And Rob was twenty yards away, being hugged by a weeping woman in a spotted blue headscarf whilst a man and a young woman thumped him on the back, grinning madly. The train had begun to shudder and hiss into action and their words were completely lost to Sylvana, although she could see their mouths all working at once. She hesitated.

Reunion

She hadn't minded that Rob had wanted to spend the first part of his leave at his parents' house. They hadn't seen him since the last time he'd been in the UK — 1968. They'd never seen Elena or met Sylvana. Rob had nearly four weeks' leave before he was to report for his new duties in Aldershot. There were no quarters currently available there so they intended to rent a house in leafy Hampshire, only an hour from Sylvana's family on the outskirts of Southampton.

Sylvana longed to see her parents again — and Lino and Tereza and the children, of course. Malta had seemed strangely empty since they'd left last spring.

Between the stay in Yorkshire and moving into the new house near Aldershot, Sylvana, Rob and Elena were to visit Gwann and Rita, Lino and Tereza, Gordon, Charles and Josie, staying with them above the restaurant, Guseppe's.

Sylvana felt a rush of joy whenever she thought of it. And Rob said it would be warmer in Southampton than in Yorkshire.

'Sylvana, this is Mam and Dad — '
Before Rob could make proper

introductions, a man with thinning sandy hair and ruddy cheeks was beside her, his face one big grin.

'Now then, lass! I'm William. And this must be Elena — ee, isn't she bonnie? I'll bet you're starved!'

The lady in the headscarf was right behind him.

'And I'm Ida, lovie. Oh, we have wanted to meet you! Will Elena come to me, do you think?' She scooped Elena up and the little girl examined the round, beaming face of her English grandmother before deciding to beam back.

'And I'm Denise!' a young woman who looked all fringe and freckles burst in. 'Our Robbie says I'm not to mither you but I've wanted to meet you for that long! You're just as pretty as your photo.'

'So are you,' Sylvana assured her young sister-in-law, smiling shyly whilst Ida and William tried to shake her hand, pick up the suitcases and loose a volley of questions about the journey. 'It's a pleasure to meet you all.'

And it was true, as all the love and

warmth that had been directed at Rob washed over Sylvana. These were Rob's people and all she wanted, at that moment, was to be taken into their home. Especially if it was warm!

His parents had done everything they could to make him and his little family welcome but Rob had forgotten how small their house was. And the plumbing was straight out of the Fifties — especially the outside lavatory!

Dad had squeezed a camp bed and a borrowed cot into Rob's old room. And, once they were alone, Sylvana looked around at the arrangement doubtfully.

'That bed is very small.'

'It's meant for a tent. It'll be OK for a fortnight.'

'I am the small one, Rob, I will sleep in the camping bed.'

He squeezed her hand.

'No, you won't! Mam would think she'd done a bad job of bringing me up if I didn't give you my old bed. I'll be fine.'

Sylvana surveyed the tiny area of floor.

'Where do we put the suitcases?'

'On the dressing-table, I suppose.' Rob pretended not to hear her sigh. He really hadn't thought much about how Mam and Dad would put them up. He wouldn't dream of hurting their feelings — but conditions were awfully cramped. It had been easier as a single man!

Hot-house Flower

All week, endless relatives swarmed in to see him and his exotic family. Although they were as welcoming as could be to Sylvana, Rob could see her growing quieter every day, hugging the fire, overwhelmed by his loud, chattering family and this freezing, wet, windy country. Even he had been shocked to wake up one morning to ferns of frost on the inside of the bedroom window-panes.

After a week, leaving Sylvana sorting clean clothes back into the suitcase, as there was nowhere else to put them, while Elena played on the bed with a jolly plastic teaset presented the evening before by Aunt Wendy, Rob ran downstairs and found his mother in the cheery yellow kitchen with black floor tiles.

'Mam, would it spoil any plans if we went out this afternoon?'

Ida turned from stirring stew on the white enamel stove, her cheeks rosy from the heat.

'Mrs Bellamy from number twenty-two will be sorry to have missed you, lovie.'

Mam could provide endless visitors to exclaim over Sylvana and Elena and tell him that he'd grown up a fine man.

'I'll say a quick hello to Mrs B., then, but we'll get off after that. I want to take Sylvana into town and it'll do Elena good to get out in the fresh air instead of being spoiled rotten by cooing relatives.'

Ida's eyes softened.

'She's that bonnie, though, Robert. And she's only here for a little while.'

'I know, Mam.' He gave her a squeeze.

'But when we're settled in Hampshire, you and Dad and our Denise will be able to come down and stop with us, won't you? It won't be like it was when I was stationed overseas. You'll be able to watch Elena grow up, at least for the next three years.'

Her grin widened until it threatened to split her face in half.

'Isn't it lovely? Do you think your Sylvana will like England?'

Judging by Sylvana's pinched little face, she wasn't enjoying it yet!

'Hope so!' he replied bracingly. 'She really wanted a home posting.'

* * *

A green double-decker bus rumbled them into town. No longer having to compete for Rob's attention, Sylvana chattered and twinkled like her old self, entranced to be sitting at the front of the top deck, peeping out over gardens.

Rob made straight for Menton's, the town centre department store that sold everything from socks to furniture, and they rode the escalator up to the first floor.

'Warm coats!' he told Sylvana. 'We'll do you and Elena first, then me.'

She squeezed his arm hard.

'Then I won't be an icicle!'

In short order, she was fitted out with a ruby red coat with a black fun fur collar that matched the cuffs, suede boots and leatherette gloves. Sylvana glowed with pleasure as she twirled before the mirror.

'I will be so warm!'

Glad to see the return of her sunny smile, he dropped a quick kiss on her pretty nose.

'My little hot-house flower.'

For Elena they chose a dark green duffel coat and brown fleece-lined boots and, for Rob, a bulky sheepskin jacket. It was dark by the time they burst back into Rob's parents' house, parking the pushchair in the hall.

Denise raced excitedly out of the living-room.

'Auntie Milly and Uncle Patrick have come, from York! Can I take Elena in, please, Sylvana? They're dying to see her.'

'Of course,' Sylvana said.

And so another round of family socialising began. But Rob was satisfied with his afternoon's work and the smile on the face of his young wife as she allowed herself to be exhibited yet again.

Elena was beautiful; everyone said so. Her dark hair curled around a smiling face and melting brown eyes. She had more energy than a monkey but Sylvana was immensely proud of her and let her show off, just a little, to her English relatives.

Auntie Milly and Uncle Patrick were more than usually doting, never having had children of their own, and Elena was soon installed on Milly's capacious lap, playing pat-a-cake.

'Ee, isn't she bonnie?' they said fondly to each other.

The family had settled to eat tea around the fire, Denise in charge of smothering hot crumpets with yellow butter, when the doorbell rang.

A Telegram

'Will you get it, William?' Ida said as she poured dark tea from a round brown teapot. William returned quickly, clutching buff paperwork and frowning fiercely.

'It's a telegram for you, Robert.'

Ida almost dropped the teapot.

'Whatever can have happened?'

'I don't see that it can be anything too awful.' Rob reached for the telegram and opened it swiftly. After a pause, he raised his eyes to Sylvana. 'I've got to report in early. The day after tomorrow.'

In a frozen moment, Sylvana felt the blood drain from her cheeks.

'Why? What will happen to the rest of your leave? Do I travel with you? Will we have somewhere to stay? Our boxes won't arrive for weeks!'

Rob's face was carefully expressionless.

'I don't really know, love. I think we'd best take the train down to Southampton tomorrow and I'll leave you with your mam and dad while I go and find out what it's all about.'

Sylvana heard her voice rising.

'Oh, Rob! We have not had much leave! And Mamma and Papa won't be expecting us yet!' Not even seeing her parents earlier than planned could make up for the prospect of Rob's leave being cut short.

'Family Is Family'

Rob reached for her hand.

'Don't take on, love. Maybe it's just that the new CO wants to meet me — '

'And what about us?' Ida burst in, clattering the teapot back on to the tin tray. 'You're supposed to be here another six days! Your life's never been your own since you joined that flaming Army, Robert!' She blinked back tears and Sylvana felt worse. Ida hadn't seen her son for three years and had obviously planned every moment of this leave with joy and anticipation. Now it was cut short.

'I know — I'm sorry, Mam. But that's what I signed up for!' Rob began to pat her hand instead of Sylvana's. 'Orders are orders.'

'But, lad!' William chimed in. 'Family is family, too!'

'I'll get the train timetable.' Sniffing, and with a carefully averted face, Denise shot through the door. Rob stared after his normally sunny sister in dismay.

Perhaps picking up on the tension, Elena began to cry. Unable to bear everyone's disappointment, Sylvana scooped her daughter up.

'She's tired. Say goodnight to everybody, Elena.' She hurried to follow Denise from the room.

Once Elena was settled in her cot, Sylvana surveyed the room they'd squashed into for the last week. Cases spilled their contents and clothes hung all around the picture rail. Slowly, she began to take the clothes down. It would be sensible to get some of the packing done before bedtime. And she thought she could hear Ida crying, downstairs. If Sylvana went back down there, she'd probably join in!

It was Rob's Army that had upset everyone. Rob could deal with it.

She had looked forward to coming to England for so long. This furlough had been planned for months: half with Rob's family and half with hers. She'd so been looking forward to Southampton next week.

But now she suspected that Rob might have to take up his new duties early. It was in his eyes. He didn't really think that the Army had sent him a telegram to call him from leave just to meet his new CO.

He was always telling her that when the Army said, 'Jump!' Rob had to reply, 'How high?' And when a woman married a soldier, she married the Army so she had to hold his hand and jump with him. But a cold hard lump in Sylvana's throat told her that she needed time on her own before she could be brave. A proper soldier's wife. She took a handkerchief from her cardigan pocket and blew her nose.

'I Understand'

It was a good job that there was a telephone at her parents' restaurant. As the heated voices coming from the living-room indicated that emotions were still high, she slipped into her new coat, pulled on her boots and went out into a bitter, frozen fog to the red telephone-box on the corner, clutching a handful of sixpences and shillings. England's red telephone-boxes were exactly like Malta's red telephone-boxes, so she had no trouble with the system. It wasn't until she heard her father's deep, 'Good evening, Guseppe's Restaurant,' that tears stole her voice.

'Papa!' she croaked.

'Sylvana! What is the matter?' He burst into swift Maltese. 'Is Elena safe? And Robert?'

'I think something's going wrong with Rob's leave.' She sniffed, blowing her nose again, feeding another shilling into the hungry slot as the 'pip, pip' in her ear told her that her first coin had been used up.

When she had explained, her father tutted.

'The Army! Yes, you must come here tomorrow. But, Sylvana, I'm sorry. We will be busy with full bookings all week. We had limited bookings for next week so that we could all spend time with you!'

Sylvana blew her nose for the last time.

'That's OK, Papa. I understand.'

'Don't Wait Up'

It took them most of the next day to travel from Yorkshire to Southampton. Sylvana tried to be cheerful but Elena was a handful on the train and even more so when they had to huddle on huge noisy stations to make connections. By the time that they climbed into a taxi in Southampton, Elena was asleep on Rob's shoulder and Sylvana wouldn't have minded a nap herself.

They drew up outside Guseppe's, gusts of rain hard against the window, and even the steamy warmth of the brightly lit restaurant across the pavement didn't really tempt Sylvana to step out of the taxi. But before she could take her daughter so that Rob could pay the taxi driver and deal with the suitcases, Gwann was standing outside with an enormous multi-coloured umbrella and a smile that lit the street.

'*Merhba!* Welcome!'

'Papa!' Sylvana scrambled for the door handle and fell into her father's warm arms, suddenly able to ignore the freezing British rain hurling itself at any exposed inch of skin.

★ ★ ★

Rob, looking so at home in khaki that it seemed he'd never been in civvies at all, left early the next morning. Sylvana rose with him, creeping around her mother's kitchen in a quilted dressing-gown, to make him eggs on toast and a cup of tea, scalding, the way he liked it. She didn't want to wake her parents. The restaurant opened until late and they hadn't been in bed long. Rain still lashed against the windows and Sylvana wondered what the weather was doing in Malta. She would have given a good deal for a mild Maltese winter's day.

Rob slid his arms around her.

'I should be back tonight. Lateish, I expect. Don't wait up — your dad's given me a key to the back door.'

Forcing a smile, Sylvana lifted her face for a kiss.

'Don't let your Army keep you away from me too long.'

He laughed.

'I'll try not to. But the Army's rather used to having things its own way.'

And then he was gone, arms swinging

and boots striking the pavement exactly as if he were on parade.

Sylvana crept back upstairs to watch him walk out of sight. Her parents had been able to give them a good big room, with a double bed and space for a cot, because the living accommodation above the restaurant seemed to go on for ever: two storeys of tall rooms and then an attic floor with gabled windows looking out over the rooftops. Rita and Gwann occupied the first floor and Lino and his family the top two.

It was too cold to stand on the uncarpeted floor to gaze out of the window, so Sylvana knelt on the bed with the eiderdown around her and gazed at the shiny wet roofs and street lights. She hadn't yet got used to the rows of tiled, sloping roofs. At home, roofs were flat and a place to dry washing or enjoy the sun.

She pulled herself up. England was home now.

She hoped that Rob's new CO would

send him straight back to his family for the remainder of his leave. Then she wouldn't complain if it rained all day, every day.

Or maybe the rain would turn to snow! She shivered. She'd never seen snow. She could help the children make a snowman with a scarf and a hat, like on Christmas cards, and she and Rob would take Lino's children out with Elena on a toboggan!

As long as the Army would let Rob have his leave.

Independence

Rita woke with a tingle of joy and apprehension. Sylvana and Elena were here! An event she'd longed for ever since the family had flown away from their beloved island. Yet she couldn't relax and enjoy it.

Instead of having the ten whole days together that they'd planned, here was Sylvana and her family six days early and unsettled by Robert's Army interfering with their plans. If Robert had to begin his duties early, as Sylvana suspected, it would be so disappointing! Sylvana would be unhappy.

Still, as she scurried across the landing in her thick dressing-gown and caught the sound of Sylvana singing to Elena, she couldn't prevent a big smile from blazing across her face. Elena was such a little doll! Last night, Rita hadn't been able to stop hugging her and gently pinching her rosy round cheeks just to hear her rich chuckles.

The restaurant wouldn't open until late afternoon and Rita was determined to take all the time she possibly could with her daughter and granddaughter.

Guseppe's was in West Parade, a row of buildings that once must have been quite grand. It had become a neighbourhood hub of commercialism with a thriving mini mart, newsagent, laundrette, pub, fruit shop and fish and chip shop.

At the other end from the fish and

chip shop, next to the fruit shop, was Guseppe's, with fresh white paintwork and a red illuminated sign. As well as the surrounding residential area — with many streets named crescent or grove, which Gwann said showed that they were in a nice district — there was a Naval training school and a Wrennery, with women tapping in and out in the smart navy uniform of the Women's Royal Navy Service.

'Good for business!' Gwann would boom as he strode in and out, attending to the orders of the diners at the tables covered with red and white tablecloths.

Rita hadn't been down in the 'family kitchen', behind the restaurant kitchen, long before Sylvana appeared, fresh and pretty in a yellow twinset and blue denim jeans. Rita hid a smile. Living with her parents in Malta, Sylvana would have felt the heat of paternal wrath if she'd thought to wear jeans. As a married woman, she was asserting her independence. And, in England, young women wore jeans! Tereza had jeans in pink and chocolate brown, as well as blue.

Tereza was fond of fashion and had a vocabulary that Rita couldn't keep up with, her tops and jumpers categorised into smocks, skinny rib and sloppy Joe. And she clumped around all day in appalling shoes called platforms that Gwann called Herman Munster shoes.

★   ★   ★

'Ah, *bambina*!' Rita held out her arms to Elena, crowing with delight when the toddler flung her arms around her neck. 'What shall Nanna give you to eat? You are a heavy girl! Perhaps I shouldn't feed you?'

Sylvana laughed, pulling out a kitchen chair.

'She won't be giving you many hugs if you don't give food to her!'

As if to prove it, Elena demanded, 'Down!' and took Rita expectantly to the fridge.

'Milk!'

During the process of settling Elena with a green plastic beaker of cold milk and setting Sylvana to slicing bread ready for buttering, Gwann wandered in, hair on end, kissing his daughter and granddaughter and taking a chair.

'The rain has stopped.'

Rita glanced at the window, surprised to see a watery sun turning the puddles to gold. She'd quite thought that January would pass in constant downpour.

'We will be able to take Sylvana and Elena out! I thought perhaps to see the big ships? We're a few miles from the sea but a bus goes straight to the docks.' She liked to see the liners that docked in Southampton. It made her feel just a touch nearer to home to know that the same ships might sometimes berth in the deep blue of Malta's Grand Harbour.

Gwann nodded.

'Gordon and Charles go to school today but Lino, Tereza and Josie will come with us. Pity it's too cold for a picnic.'

Sylvana peered out at the sky over the

orderly yard containing bins and boxes, a wooden trolley and a sack barrow.

'I would prefer to go for a walk. I seem to have spent weeks on planes, trains and buses! And Elena needs to play. Rob bought her wellingtons and she would love to splash.'

'The recreation ground, then!' Rita began putting jams and cheeses out on the breakfast table. 'We can walk there with the pushchair and then Elena can get out, where it's safe.' Her attention switched swiftly to the window. 'Ian is in our yard, Gwann! What is he staring at?'

Attractive

Gwann jumped up and opened the back door into the walled yard. '*Alio! Ian!*'

After watching the two men talking and gazing upward for a minute, Rita turned back to the table.

'We will eat. Papa will come in soon.'

Sylvana added sugar to her coffee.

'Who is Ian? Is he Papa's friend?'

'He owns the fruit shop next door and he's our landlord. His father bought his building and also this building and left them to Ian. We rent this one and he uses that one for his shop.'

Brown eyes turned on her enquiringly.

'Your landlord! Does he interfere like this every day?'

'I don't think he's here to interfere. He's a nice young man,' Rita protested. But Gwann was beginning to throw his arms around and perch his hands upon his hips as he did when he was indignant.

Rita hoped Gwann would remember that Ian owned the roof over their heads. He seemed so young to them that Gwann might try bossing him about.

'It looks as if Papa is bringing him in here.' Rita rose to refill the coffee percolator.

Then Gwann and Ian were in the kitchen, wiping their feet on the coconut matting and blowing on their hands, bringing with them the fresh scent of outdoors.

'I'm sorry, Gwann. But that's what 'repairing lease' means,' Ian was saying. 'And you can see why it won't wait.'

Gwann frowned, yet motioned for Ian to take a seat at the big kitchen table. Automatically, Rita placed a cup and saucer in front of him.

'Coffee will be ready in five minutes.' Ian smiled.

'I'm interrupting your breakfast — I'm sorry. But that coffee smells too good for me to refuse, even though I'm the bearer of bad tidings. I'm afraid one of the cast iron downpipes has snapped and water is pouring from it and off your outhouse roof into my yard. It's pouring against the wall, too, so it won't be long before it's making your bedrooms damp on the second floor.' He sounded apologetic.

'And we must fix,' Gwann succinctly added.

Rita knew that they were responsible for repairs — and she knew that Gwann knew that, too! But Gwann, before getting on with it, must have his grumble.

She returned Ian's smile. She liked the cheerful young man with his curly hair and sea blue eyes, even though his hair tumbled well past his collar, his wardrobe seemed inspired by the rainbow and he wore chunky silver necklaces around his throat.

Having inherited well, he could have let out the property next door and lived off his rents but, instead, he worked hard in his own shop.

Before she could ask exactly what a downpipe was, Ian had turned to Sylvana.

'Hello! You must be one of the Bonnici family I haven't met before. I'm Ian Mortimer from the fruit shop.'

Politely, Sylvana took his extended hand.

'I am Sylvana.' She hesitated, then added, 'Sylvana Denton. This is my daughter, Elena.'

Rita smiled. Judging by the disappointment that flickered over Ian's face,

Sylvana had sensed that Ian needed to have it made plain that she was a married woman. With the winter sunlight picking out the copper lights in Sylvana's thick, lustrous hair, her creamy skin and trim figure, she certainly did look attractive and it was no surprise that she should encounter an admiring man.

But Rita was glad to see that her daughter knew how to sidestep him.

Family Life

It was such a pleasure to be out in the sunshine! Even if it was British winter sunshine, accompanied by sharp-edged gusts that turned fingers and toes to ice. The recreation ground — known as the Rec — with a square-towered church looking over the treetops at benches edging pathways around formal lawns, netball and tennis courts, was an oasis in the suburbs of the city. Sylvana felt as if she could smell the luscious grass. There was hardly any grass in Malta and the dark green *kappara* that took a toehold in any rocky crevice smelled much different.

Lino and Gwann had stayed to try to effect a temporary repair on the rogue downpipe and so only Sylvana, Rita and Tereza wheeled the pushchairs up to the children's play park. Tereza, obviously already used to the local climate, wore a crocheted hat, scarf and gloves, boots, jeans and a thickly embroidered sheepskin coat.

'So, what do you think of Southampton? Do you like the restaurant? What about the weather?' Her hair whipped free of the hat, across her eyes.

Holding Elena firmly, Sylvana hopped on a roundabout like a big shuttlecock and settled her daughter on her lap.

'Everything's lovely — except the weather! I want to live here but I'll have to grow another skin. A furry one!'

Because Tereza laughed, Sylvana didn't add that this was what her mother-in-law had said when she saw the new coat and boots that Rob had bought Sylvana.

Rob's telegram, unfortunately, had transformed Ida from smiling hostess to disappointed fault-finder.

Tereza wrinkled her nose.

'Because we arrived in springtime we've been able to get used to the weather gradually. I feel sorry for you arriving in the winter! And the weather forecast says it will soon get colder.'

'Have you seen snow?' Sylvana pushed at the ground with her foot to make the roundabout speed up.

'Not enough to cover the ground.' Tereza sighed. 'But Gordon and Charles pray for snow so deep that they won't be able to go to school but will be able to go outside and build a snowman.'

Rita came over from the seesaw, clutching Josie by the hand, and perched herself beside them as the roundabout slowed.

'The trouble with snow is that it's cold!' She shivered theatrically.

'So.' Sylvana pushed with her foot again, as Elena seemed content to watch the world spinning by. 'Are you glad you came to England?'

'It's a good place.' Rita nodded seriously. 'We can earn a living. The children go to a good school and our neighbours are friendly. There's not enough sunshine, it's not Malta, but maybe we won't be here for ever.'

The roundabout slowed and, this time, Sylvana let it, before the spinning had an unfortunate effect on Elena's tummy.

'We've become quite a travelling family.'

After they'd picked up the older children, Gordon and Charles, from school, who immediately loaded their satchels on to the pushchairs, they walked back to West Parade. The streetlights were already coming on as a now cloudless sky darkened and the temperature plummeted. Sylvana tucked a blanket around Elena.

Back in the warmth of the family kitchen she made dinner for all four children, to free the adults to change and hurry into the restaurant kitchen ready for the six o'clock opening. Tired from their afternoon in the fresh air, Josie and Elena bickered over a tower of coloured beakers, Gordon and Charles sighed over their homework and Sylvana wondered when Rob would come home. And what his CO had said.

Long Day

After the children had eaten, Tereza rushed into the kitchen, a frilled white apron around her neat black dress.

'You're an angel, Sylvana! Gordon, Charles, go and wash, then change into your pyjamas, please. You can watch TV upstairs until eight-thirty. No! No arguing! I don't care what's on until nine, bedtime is eight-thirty on a school night.'

Next in was Rita, using her twenty-minute break to drink coffee and slide her shoes off beneath the table with a sigh.

'Shall I begin dinner for the adults?' Sylvana asked, acutely aware that

109

everyone else was working in the family business.

Rita waved an airy hand.

'We'll eat off the menu tonight. We do that a couple of times a week. Will you wait for Robert to come home before you eat?'

Sylvana looked at the kitchen clock for the millionth time, wishing that it could tell her the result of Rob's day in Aldershot.

'I don't know how late he'll be. I'll wait for a while.'

In fact, by the time Rob finally walked across the yard, his breath a cloud in the night air, Sylvana was standing in her dressing-gown and slippers, waiting for the kettle to boil for a hot-water bottle, and talking to Gwann, who was eating his meal in his chef whites. She unlocked the back door before Rob reached it.

'I thought you were lost! You are very cold. What did they say? Did you meet your new CO?'

Rob gave her a big hug.

'I'm frozen and I'm hungry.'

Obviously, he didn't want to talk in front of her father! Sylvana broke free of his embrace with a smile that disguised the hurrying of her heart.

'Would sir like to see a menu?'

'No dressing-gowns in my restaurant kitchen,' Gwann stipulated. 'Rob choose, I fetch it.'

★ ★ ★

It was almost an hour before Sylvana and Rob could decently withdraw to the privacy of their room, an hour when Sylvana hugged her hot-water bottle and watched Rob and her father eat, as if there was no burning need inside her to drag answers out of Rob. She pretended that she hadn't noticed that Rob seemed to have difficulty meeting her gaze.

But at last they were able to say goodnight and Sylvana rushed though the staircases and corridors to their room, teeth chattering after the warmth of the kitchen. She hopped straight beneath the covers.

Rob's News

'They've said you have to start straight away, haven't they?'

'No,' Rob said slowly. 'I can have the rest of my leave.'

He sat down on the side of the bed and took her hand, the khaki serge rough against her skin, his buttons shining. He kissed her hand and smiled oddly.

'But I've been given fresh orders and at the end of my leave I have to report to Government Communications HQ in Cheltenham for briefing.'

Sylvana felt a smile of relief burst across her face.

'So everything is all right? Just that your job has changed.'

Rob didn't smile.

'Well — it's not a 'just' sort of change. I'm to take a team of technicians out to Gan Island in the Maldives for six months.

We'll be attached to an RAF base.' His eyes were fixed on Sylvana.

'Oh.' She examined this new information. 'So we won't move into the house near Aldershot?'

He shook his head.

'No point, really.'

'At least it's warm in the Maldives!' She smiled suddenly. 'I wanted to come to the UK but it is awfully cold. I won't be too upset to be posted elsewhere. It will be summer in six months, when we come back!'

Slowly, Rob reached out and stroked her cheek.

'It's a single posting, Sylvana. No families. Just me.'

4

July 1971

By the time he reached RAF Lyneham in England, Rob was thoroughly sick of travelling. This trip home from Gan Island had seemed a particularly convoluted one, through Singapore, Tripoli and Cyprus.

But only transport to the station remained and then Rob could jump on a blessedly civilian train to Southampton. And Sylvana.

He drank in the greens and golds of rural Wiltshire and breathed the July breeze as the driver secured his baggage and that of his men.

'Just like at RAF Gan, we're getting stares for being Army boys intruding on an RAF base, but at least this one isn't in the middle of nowhere so that pilots overlook it and fly right over,' Rob joked.

Air traffic and fresh faces at RAF Gan had been depressingly low. Once a busy staging post for the RAF, now it served mainly as a radar, communications and weather station.

Soames, his corporal, grinned.

'Can't blame them. There wasn't much for us to do but look at palm trees, fish, complain about the heat and to remember what women look like. Ready when you are, Staff.' The impatience in his eyes belied the respect in his voice.

Rob clapped him on the shoulder.

'Then let's get off on leave.'

Because Rob was in uniform the taxi driver refused to charge the fare from Southampton railway station to Guseppe's Restaurant.

'No, mate,' he declared. 'I did me national service in the Army and I ain't taking a bean off of you.'

Rob was so busy calling surprised thanks as the busy cabbie sped off into the twilight that it took him several seconds to realise that Guseppe's wasn't open for business. No light spilled through the plate glass on to the pavement or illuminated the menu encased beside the door. No diners laughed and chatted at the tables, no silverware or glasses winked in the candlelight.

Hoisting up his luggage, Rob hurried round to the gate and through the back yard, and saw that all the living quarters above the restaurant were in darkness, too.

He'd been deliberately vague about his time of arrival so that Sylvana wouldn't be disappointed if he was held up. He knew he was a full day earlier than his conservative estimate, but it had never occurred to him that he'd find the place deserted.

He fumbled for his key and burst through the kitchen door.

'Sylvana!' Fear pinched his stomach. 'Sylvana, are you here? Gwann? Rita?'

Silence was his only answer.

Racing up to his and Sylvana's room, he found the double bed was made neatly and a small, tumbled bed with a pink candlewick bedspread reminded him that his daughter was now too big for a cot.

He put his hands to the sheets. They were cold. Slowly, he dropped his kit on the floor.

Back downstairs, everything in both the family kitchen and the restaurant kitchen was cold, too. It had clearly been some time since the family had cooked a meal or boiled a kettle.

Rob sat down at the kitchen table, baffled. The realisation that he had no idea of the whereabouts of his wife and daughter settled like ice around his heart. And where was the crowd of in-laws that normally bustled around the place? It was just like an old black-and-white film he'd seen, back on Gan Island, when a flying saucer had sent down tractor beams to suck whole families from their houses.

He dropped his head in his hands.

But, in a moment, he was back on his feet, moving methodically through the rooms, checking — in vain — for a note with his name on it.

Rob had a whole hour to wait alone in the silence, pacing from window to window to stare out at the darkness before, finally, he heard the rattle of the back gate and sprinted down the stairs.

'Call The Police!'

Sylvana shivered in the night air, more from shock than from cold. 'I don't want to leave her for long.' She tried to find a dry corner of her handkerchief to dab her eyes.

'You heard what the doctors said.' Ian's voice came through the darkness, warm and reassuring. 'She's in good hands and the danger's past. You'll be more use to her after a good night's sleep than if you keep a bedside vigil.'

'A 'totally unnecessary' vigil,' she corrected him indignantly, quoting the doctor. She managed a watery smile of thanks as Ian held the gate open for her.

Ian laughed softly.

'I'm sure his intentions were good.'

In the darkness, as they walked round from Ian's yard to their own, Sylvana felt her mother's arm slip through hers.

'She'll get better soon, Sylvana. You know what children are like. A few days and she'll be running everywhere, as usual.'

'I hope so.' Sylvana halted. 'Did we leave the lights on in the kitchen?'

Her father stepped in her path.

'I'll go first. Somebody has unlocked the door.'

Ian eased past Sylvana, too, suddenly holding himself very tall.

'I'll go in with you, Gwann.'

Sylvana felt unshed tears tightening her throat, her voice high with the emotion of the last few hours.

'Papa, no, please call the police!' And she tried to push through the doorway, tangling her arms with Ian's as she reached for her father, who was stalking into his home like a cowboy at high noon.

Then they all froze as a figure shot

into the room from the hall, khaki shirt open at the neck.

A Joyous Event

'Rob!' Uncaring of her dignity — or anybody's toes — Sylvana fought free of the crush in the doorway and launched herself across the room, her arms outstretched. 'Rob, Elena has been so ill. We take her to the hospital because she cannot breathe — '

Rob, in the midst of opening his arms to his wife, grabbed her by the shoulders.

'She wasn't breathing?'

'She was breathing, but not good . . .' Sylvana's English completely deserted her. The whole frightening episode became too much and she melted against Rob's broad chest and broke down into a storm of tears.

Ian clarified diffidently.

'Elena had an asthma attack. She's had a chesty cold and then began to wheeze. We took her to hospital in my car and they were able to sort her out quite quickly with an injection and they've begun antibiotics for a chest infection. But they want to keep her in for a day or two.'

'And they won't let me stay with her.' Sylvana emerged from the warmth of Rob's shirt. 'They say she must be kept very quiet tonight and I should not return to the hospital until morning.'

Rob's arms tightened around Sylvana, his voice hoarse in her ear.

'Our poor little girl! We'll go together. Don't worry, love. She can't be in any danger if they sent you home.'

Sylvana felt herself begin to relax. She'd been so scared when Elena had been fighting for breath, her little chest seeming to sink in her efforts to fill her lungs, that she'd almost forgotten the joyous event of Rob coming home. She straightened suddenly.

'You are home early!'

'Yes, I was meant to be a nice surprise.' He reached past her, to Ian. 'I'm grateful to you for helping my wife and my daughter. Thank you.' He shook Ian's hand.

'You're welcome,' Ian replied, his kind face creasing into a smile. 'Goodnight, then, everyone.' He grinned quickly at Sylvana and then disappeared into the darkness outside.

'Thank you!' Sylvana tried to call after his retreating back, but the door was closing and everyone was talking at once, Rob asking questions about Elena's illness and Gwann and Rita asking Rob about his journey back to the UK.

'Sit And Eat'

As Rob responded politely, Sylvana had the chance to study him. He looked tired, his hair on end, his eyes blue against his tan. Gan Island had been very hot, he'd said in all his letters. Not dry and hot, like Malta, but so humid that it felt as if he should be drinking the air rather than breathing it.

She realised suddenly that Gwann and

Rita were doing what she should have been doing — sitting Rob down at the kitchen table and finding him something to eat and drink. But barely had she made her first movement towards the big white fridge in the corner than her mother stood in her way.

'Sit down!'

'But Rob — '

'Yes, Robert is tired and hungry. And so are we all. No restaurant tonight, so we all sit down together and get over our fright while Elena sleeps safe in the hospital. Tonight, I cook, you eat — no argument, Sylvana. Sit with your husband.'

Meekly, Sylvana did as she was told, reaching out across the table to take Rob's hand.

The blue eyes fixed on her.

'Can you tell me exactly what happened?' His voice was gentle but his frown of concentration reminded Sylvana that he was a man used to assessing situations and taking any necessary action. The thought gave her a sudden feeling of warmth inside. Poor little Elena's illness didn't seem quite so bad with Rob there to share the worry with her.

So, as Rita bustled around with a quick meal of potatoes and cauliflower to go with a cold cut of pork from the fridge, Sylvana found herself retracing every petrifying moment of the day, trembling as the images of Elena's struggle and the controlled urgency of the medical staff chased one another through her memory.

Gently, Rob took her through the whole day, wheedling out of her details that she hadn't even known she'd forgotten. Gwann and Rita chipped in, too, until Rob was in possession of most of the facts.

'Thank goodness you all acted so promptly and that Elena's safe.' He squeezed Sylvana's fingers. 'I couldn't imagine what had happened when I saw the restaurant was shut. Where are Lino and Tereza and the boys?'

'In Malta, for the wedding of Tereza's sister, Mary,' Sylvana reminded him. 'I wrote to you about this.'

'Of course you did, I'd forgotten.

So what about Ian? How did he get involved?'

'Ian! Thank goodness for Ian! Papa ran next door to ask Ian to take us to the hospital in his car. And he came into the hospital with us because we were all forgetting our English, we were so scared. He was wonderful,' she added fervently.

Rob frowned.

Journey To Hospital

In the morning, Sylvana was woken by twin sensations of unfamiliarity and anxiety. It took her several seconds to trace the origins of the feelings, until she realised that Rob was beside her in bed — but that Elena's bed was empty. And when she looked at the cream-coloured alarm clock she didn't need the luminous feature of its dial, because it was almost eight in the morning.

She bolted upright.

Instantly, Rob was awake beside her. 'What?'

'Elena! I have overslept. They said I could return to the children's ward at nine. Ian will be expecting me at half-past eight.'

Rob swung his legs out of bed.

'We don't need to bother Ian. We can make our own way to the hospital.'

Sylvana shook her head as she reached for clean clothes.

'No, it is arranged already. It is two buses to the hospital from here but only twenty minutes in the car.' She washed and dressed quickly, brushed her long hair and shot downstairs.

'We haven't eaten,' Rob objected, catching up with her as she reached for the kitchen door. 'You won't help Elena if you're fainting through lack of food. A soldier marches on his belly, you know.'

Sylvana stared.

'What does that mean?'

He smiled suddenly, the white laughter lines beside his eyes creasing into his tan, and she realised that she hadn't seen many smiles from him since he'd been home.

'It means you're going to have something to eat before you go. A jam butty will do.'

Sylvana giggled.

'Nobody has made me a jam butty while you've been away.'

He made a face of mock horror.

'That's no way to run an army. Come on, let's have a jam butty and a cup of char. Elena will be fine for another few minutes, after all.'

Rob was very good at the efficient preparation and consumption of a basic meal and they were only five minutes late letting themselves into Ian's yard.

The journey to the hospital frightened Sylvana much less than the day before, now that Rob was sitting beside her on the back seat of Ian's big grey Rover, holding her hand, quiet but assured in his neat civvy sports jacket, distinguished from Ian and other civilian men by the precision of his short-back-and-sides haircut compared with their manes of hair.

Ian's dark hair was curling madly over

his open collar and, next to Rob, he looked what Gwann termed 'a bit of a hippy' with his neck chain and the embroidery on his jeans. But his way-out style didn't prevent him from being a good man.

'Shall I wait?' Ian suggested, as he eased his car into the hospital car park.

'We've put you to quite enough trouble,' Rob said easily. 'Thank you very much indeed.'

He shook Ian's hand, waited until Sylvana had said her farewells and then tucked her hand into the crook of his arm.

'I can't wait to see my little girl.'

'I can see that! I have to run to keep up.' Sylvana laughed as he strode rapidly towards the row of glass doors that marked the entrance to the wards.

'Look Who's Here!'

It was a huge relief to find Elena sitting on her bed, undressing a one-armed doll and talking to herself. But when she saw Sylvana and Rob, her face crumpled and her dark eyes began to spill shining tears.

A nurse grinned at Sylvana reassuringly as, with a cluck of distress, Sylvana gathered her daughter into her arms.

'Don't worry — they all do that. Once they get Mum back they go to bits for five minutes. She'll be fine.'

Sylvana snuggled the little head into her neck.

'Don't be sad. Look — who have I brought to see you? It's Daddy!'

Instantly, Elena's tears ceased. She fixed big brown eyes on Rob but kept her little arm tight around her mother.

'Hello, Elena,' Rob said, his smile misty as he folded gentle fingers around his daughter's hand. 'I've been looking for you everywhere. Fancy me finding you here in hospital.' He pulled a funny face and Elena gave a watery giggle.

In minutes Elena was perched upon his knee as if he'd never been away, wanting him to dress the doll — so that she could promptly undress it — and all but ignoring the doctor who arrived to examine her, merely piping, 'No!' and trying to bat away the stethoscope.

'Be a good girl, Elena,' Rob said gravely. 'The doctor needs to hear whether your breathing is better. Let him listen to your chest.'

With a sigh and a look at her father under her lashes, Elena submitted to the chill of the stethoscope, clutching her doll in one hand and Rob's big thumb in the other.

The doctor was a rounded, grey-haired man with a toothbrush moustache.

'Well, young lady, you're much better,' he pronounced. 'I think we're going to be able to let Mummy and Daddy take you home now.' He turned to Rob. 'Small children — they bounce back like rubber balls. I wouldn't believe that this is the same little girl who was so poorly yesterday.'

Anxiety shadowed Rob's face.

'But you're sure she's well enough to leave?'

'With medicine to take with her, yes. And a visit to her own doctor in a few days, just to see how she's going along. She might never have another asthma attack, some children don't. Keep her quiet for a few days.'

Elena Comes Home

A taxi was the sensible way to get home from the hospital. Rob wouldn't hear of troubling Ian to come and fetch them.

'I'm sure he's been really kind,' he said, 'but I want to look after my own family, now I'm here. You can understand that, love, can't you?'

'But he's expecting me to phone,' Sylvana protested. Then she shrugged. 'You're right. I'll go and tell him when we're home. He'll want to know how Elena is — he was very worried on Friday night.'

'I'll do it. Elena will want her mummy home with her.'

So Sylvana turned her attention to

making Elena sit still on the back seat between her parents. The doctor who had said Elena ought to be kept quiet should try making her!

It wasn't until mid-afternoon, when Elena, tiring abruptly, went to sleep on her mummy's shoulder, that Sylvana was able to pay Rob any real attention. He followed her up into their room as she stooped to transfer their daughter to her little bed, frowning over the heat of Elena's skin.

With a sigh, Sylvana turned to her husband, winding her arms around his neck.

'Sometimes, being a mother is frightening.'

He nodded.

'A father, too. I almost went off my head when I came home and there was nobody here.' He paused to drop kisses on Sylvana's nose. 'I've spent most of the last months thinking about coming home to you.'

'Next time, I will make . . . what is that thing? Oh, yes! A welcome committee!' she teased him, laughing into his blue eyes.

'That would be much nicer. Be here, with hugs and kisses — I didn't know who to worry about first, when the place was empty.'

She wrinkled her nose.

'Don't worry about me. I am healthy — apart from the fear in my heart when my daughter was wheezing so much. I am better now.' She glanced at her watch. 'I should be helping in the kitchen whilst Elena sleeps, but I am going to stay with her, just for today. Mama agrees but I feel bad, with Lino and Tereza already away.'

Rob's brows lifted.

'Do you normally work in the kitchen?'

She tutted.

'I write this to you, Rob. I work in the kitchen and in the restaurant and share the caring of the children with Mama and Tereza.'

'I remember now. You've really settled in here.' He hesitated. 'I went round and thanked your friend Ian for the help he gave to you. He's obviously a very helpful chap.'

A prickle of disquiet ran up Sylvana's back.

'He is a friend of all the family.'

'I think he's particularly friendly with you.'

Sylvana drew away a little.

'He is a friend of all the family,' she repeated firmly.

Rob's gaze was steady.

'Well. I'm here now, so he can be my friend, too.'

Slowly, Sylvana unwound her arms from around Rob's neck.

'I expect he will.'

*   *   *

It was a strange day. Not the first day home that Rob had anticipated. Instead of the — well, yes, the welcome committee! — that he'd dreamed of for months, he found his daughter's temper fluctuated with her temperature and she was apt to cling to her mother, who

134

was completely preoccupied with her little charge.

By the time Elena finally gave in to sleep, her hair sticking in damp tendrils to her flushed face, Sylvana could scarcely speak for her yawns, after a week of disturbed nights.

Rob didn't share her fatigue — he'd hardly done anything all day but drift around the house — so he cleared a pile of Elena's clothes from the small, hard armchair in the corner of their bedroom and settled down with a newspaper. He and Sylvana had no sitting-room of their own — Sylvana usually used the big family kitchen as living space when she wasn't in the bedroom or working.

Whilst he was grateful to Gwann and Rita for their hospitality, living in the pockets of his in-laws would take some getting used to after the men-only atmosphere of Gan Island — and, anyway, he wanted to be near his wife and daughter.

Elena still wheezed a little and he found himself listening to the regular

135

squeaky breaths instead of concentrating on an account of the launch of the Apollo 15 spacecraft.

A clattering from the restaurant kitchen reached him faintly, and the occasional ringing of the telephone. Apart from that, with Lino and Tereza and their children away and Rita and Gwann rushed off their feet downstairs, the residential floors were quiet.

Exciting News

'What were you going to tell me?' Sylvana's voice came suddenly across the room, making him jump.

'When?'

'You wrote to me that when you came home, you would have news about your posting.'

Rob put the paper on the floor and crossed to sit beside her on the bed, glad she hadn't plummeted into sleep the instant her head met the pillow.

'That's right! Quite exciting stuff.'

His heart rate picked up in anticipation of finally sharing his news with her.

She looked up at him and smiled, the lines of strain fading now that Elena was comfortably asleep.

'Is the home posting confirmed?'

He hesitated.

'Well, yes and no. There is a home posting in the wind, but it's only provisional.'

Her finely arched brows drew down over her eyes in a puzzled frown as she absorbed his words.

'So there is another posting available for you? Hong Kong? Or Germany?'

He lifted her hand and kissed it.

'No. I think I'm going to buy myself out. Leave the Army. I've been offered a smashing job in Canada. And I think I'm going to take it because it looks really interesting.'

She sat up, eyes wide.

'What kind of job? Why don't you want the home posting? Is it a very bad position that they offer you in the UK?'

'No,' he acknowledged. 'No, I think it

would be a very good position, with a promotion.'

'And with a quarter?'

'Probably.' He hesitated, aware that Sylvana's eyes weren't shining at the thought of a new job in Canada. There was no flush of pleasure or rush of delighted questions. Her eyes were fixed on him, all right, but their expression was more of consternation than happiness.

'Look, love,' he said awkwardly, stroking her hand. 'The job in Canada won't be any different from any Army posting. You and Elena will come with me and we'll have a home, all together. I think I'd like to be a civilian again. Wear what I want, let my hair grow into a mad mess, like all the other blokes do.'

'What About Us?'

Sylvana dropped her eyes. She fussed with her pillows, removing her hand from his and propping herself up so that she could see his face.

'But, also, we could live in the UK, and you have a very good job and promotion.'

'Well . . . yes.' He smiled. 'If we want that.'

'I want that,' she said, dark eyes fixed intensely to his. 'I want what I've always wanted — to be with you and live in a married quarter and be happy.'

'Love,' he responded gently. 'It's not always like it was in Malta. That was a cushy posting for me and we got a lovely quarter because most of the services had vacated. Here, it would probably be in an enormous barracks and not such a good quarter. The post they're offering has got a lot more desk work to it — which isn't very exciting. I'm not sure that I want to be stuck here in a pretty ordinary job in the UK and I'm a bit tired of the Army telling me what to do. It's a great job that I've been offered in Canada.'

Her voice was small.

'Tell me about the job. You want to

take it, obviously.'

He captured her hand again.

'It's too good an opportunity to miss, love.'

Drawing herself up against the pillows, Sylvana stiffened.

'You've taken the job?'

'No!' he protested. 'I'm just telling you that I want to take it.'

After several frowning moments, Sylvana spoke.

'So, if you go to Canada, where will I be? And Elena? In a house in a town? Or a village? Or a city?'

Rob smiled and tried to recapture some of the enthusiasm that had been burning inside him for the last couple of weeks.

'We can pretty much choose. I'll be working four weeks on and two weeks off, so we can base ourselves in any number of places.'

'I don't understand this four weeks and two weeks.'

'Sorry, I'm not being very clear. The job is to bring new telecommunications networks to a huge swathe of rural Canada — there are several patches up for grabs so I can't be more specific at the moment. I'd be travelling, doing that, for four weeks. Then I'd come home for two weeks. Then off for four weeks again, and so on.'

Sylvana was silent.

'Canada's a great country. Elena will love it.'

Restlessly, Sylvana rose, glancing down at him.

'How do you know what your daughter loves? You've been away for more than half her life.'

Melodramatic

She picked up her clothes. 'Sorry, but I go to work now. I need to think about what to do. You are here, on leave, to watch over Elena, so it's not good to leave Mama and Papa to struggle downstairs. I'm going now, to help.'

Rob felt his colour rising.

'Wouldn't it be better to stay here and talk about this?'

Sylvana turned away.

'I have to think about what you propose for me and Elena. Taking her away from the family who loves her — the family she knows.'

Rob followed Sylvana across the room, alarmed to see teardrops trembling on her long lashes. Gently, he slid his arms around her.

'You're being very melodramatic. I didn't mean to make you upset.'

She sighed.

'Really, I'm not upset. I'm just thinking that maybe I'll stay here and you can visit. Just like before. It seems the most sensible option, if we're only to be living together for one-third of the year anyway.'

Living Apart

Rita spread her newspaper across the yellow melamine-topped kitchen table, enjoying a cup of coffee as she devoured the copy of 'The Times Of Malta' that Tereza and Lino had brought home with them on the plane.

Even though it was mid-morning, not one of Lino's family had yet come downstairs after arriving from the airport in the middle of the night, so she could luxuriate in the news about the new hotels in St George's Bay and how Sliema Wanderers were doing in the run-up to the football season.

She looked up only when there was a knock on the back door.

'Hello!' She waved Ian in, simultaneously reaching for the coffee percolator. 'Do you come to see Gwann? He is arguing with the fish delivery man. He does not think English fish is as fresh as Maltese fish.'

Ian sat down.

'I don't suppose it is, to be fair. A cup of your delicious coffee would be wonderful. If he hasn't appeared by the time I've drunk it, I'll come back later. Oh — hello, Sylvana! How's Elena?'

Sylvana gave him a big smile as she entered the room.

'She is much better now, Ian.' She took down a cup and saucer and reached for the percolator as she told him all about Elena's return to health. Rita, who hadn't missed the pleasure on Ian's face at the sight of Sylvana, realised that Sylvana had smiled at Ian more in five minutes than she had smiled at Rob in five days. A worm of worry wriggled inside her.

'Time for work,' she said suddenly, with a decisive nod. 'Sylvana, the clean overalls and aprons are folded in the basket.'

Immediately, Ian leapt to his feet, as Rita had known he would.

'I mustn't keep you, if you're busy.' And he was gone in a twinkling.

Sylvana looked disconsolate.

'I haven't finished my coffee.'

'But if we hurry this morning, we can find an hour to take the children out this afternoon. With Rob.' Rita gave her daughter a wide, beaming smile.

Gwann was deeply troubled. His son-in-law had been home for a week now, but where was the joy that should have returned with him?

He watched his daughter, moving silently around the kitchen, her hair held in a net, her face troubled.

'You know,' he began, 'we Maltese have always found ourselves scattered around the world. We're a small country and we must adapt when it's necessary.'

Sylvana didn't pretend that she didn't know what he was driving at.

'But it's not necessary. He could have a home posting.'

There was a long silence, broken only by the sound of Gwann's chef's knife rat-a-tatting on the board as he chopped onions.

'Papa, thank you for not saying it.'

'Not saying what?'

'That I brought this trouble on myself by marrying a soldier.'

Gwann twinkled across at her.

'This is nothing to do with the Army.' She sniffed.

'I've told Rob that I might stay here. Will you let me?'

Throwing down his knife, Gwann crossed the distance between them, pulling her against him and letting her tears soak into his chef whites. Nothing in his experience as a father had prepared him for this horrible situation.

'I would never refuse you a place in my house.' But his voice was laced with uneasiness.

'You don't think I'm doing the right thing?'

Disappointment was evident through her tears.

He sighed.

'I don't know. I just don't know.'

Sylvana didn't answer.

Much later, when the restaurant blinds were down and the building almost silent, Gwann found Rob in the family kitchen.

Gwann grunted.

'Ah — you join me for late-night coffee?'

Rob shrugged. He looked tired and uncomfortable, as if he felt out of place. Plugging in the percolator, Gwann glanced Rob's way.

'Sylvana, she asked me if she can stay here, with Elena, when you go to Canada,' he said baldly.

Rob looked up, suddenly alert.

'That means she'll come with me if you tell her that she can't stay here.'

'That's possible.' Gwann rubbed his chin. 'Or she could return to Malta.'

Rob stared.

'Her brother and sister are still there. Most of her family,' Gwann reminded him.

Rob's voice sounded unsteady.

'But shouldn't wife and husband be together?'

'Almost always.' Gwann took down two cups and saucers from the glass-fronted cupboard on the wall and spoke gently.

'Robert, never in my family do I know a wife who does not live with her husband. I don't like my daughter to be

147

the first one. But — ' He gave a shrug. 'But this is the marriage you offer Sylvana: 'I am a soldier. Always, we live here, we live there.'

'But, in reality, there has been no 'we', has there? Always it has been Sylvana here, Robert there. Now you come and tell her that you have chosen a new job. In the words that you use very often, that is not what Sylvana signed up for. And you have shown Sylvana very well how to live here while you live there.'

'Am I Wrong?'

The percolator bubbled and popped, filling the room with steamy coffee fragrance, while Rob digested Gwann's speech.

'The job in Canada is a good opportunity.'

Gwann let out a sigh. Rob had gone about selling a new life in Canada to Sylvana in entirely the wrong way.

It wasn't really his fault. During the three years of his marriage, he'd only actually been in it for about ten months. The rest of the time he'd been living as a single man, called upon every day to be decisive and act on his own initiative. It wasn't the best training for the give and take of marriage.

Gwann rose and poured the coffee into the cups.

'I'm not going to tell my daughter that there's no home for her here, Robert. I tell her what I tell you — I am very sad and sorry that you are thinking of living apart.'

Rob's eyes darkened.

'So you think I'm wrong to want to go to Canada?'

Gwann blew calmly across the surface of his coffee.

'My question is — do you think you are right?'

5

August 5, 1971

Dear Robert,

Thank you for your letter, dear, but I must say it has given us all something to chew on. We were so looking forward to you and Sylvana and Elena living in England for a while, and being able to visit you, as you said when you first came home from Malta. Before that idea went for a burton, because the Army sent you to Gan Island. I used to think that if you wrote to say you were leaving the Army I'd be thrilled, but I had no idea it would mean you upping sticks to live halfway around the world, instead. Canada's such a long way . . .

'Robert? Your mother is asking for you on the telephone.'

As he looked up from the letter on the kitchen table, Rob blinked at Gwann, switching his thoughts with an effort from his mother's neat handwriting to the peculiar notion that she might be asking for him on the telephone.

'Mam? On the phone? She hates phones. I've never spoken to her on a phone in my life.' She had been steadfast in her refusal to have a phone installed in their house, to the eternal disgust of his sister, Denise.

He looked at Gwann's grave expression and an uncomfortable feeling began to uncoil itself in his stomach.

Gwann stood back, as if encouraging Rob to leave the room.

'Urgent, she says.'

Rob unfroze, brushing past his father-in-law and darting up the hall into the area he rarely had cause to enter, a little cubicle at the back of the restaurant with a black telephone on a desk beside a grey cash register. He snatched up the handset. As soon as he jammed it to his ear he could hear Ida's anxious breathing.

'Mam? What's up?'

'Robert! Oh, my word, Robert, it's your dad. It wasn't his fault, it was someone else took a shortcut in the safety procedure but it was him that got a face full. I don't know what to do with myself, he's so bad. Our Denise is here but she doesn't know what to do, either.'

Ida's voice rose in panic.

Rob fought to keep his voice even.

'It's all right, Mam. If something's happened to Dad, I'll come and help you. Just slow down and tell me what it is.'

It took several moments and some strident nose-blowing before Ida's wobbly voice would work again.

'Your dad was at the factory and there was some kind of explosion. You know the kind of stuff he works with — batteries and that. And he copped for a load of fragments, right in his face, love. Oh . . . ' She had to pause to blow her nose again. 'Robert — it's all in his eyes! His eyes! They don't know if they can save his sight.'

'Oh, no!' Heart beating so loudly he could hardly hear his own voice, Rob gripped the cold black Bakelite of the phone, calling on all his Army training to make himself detach, to thrust aside emotion and focus on action. 'Is he in much pain?'

'Not so much now he's in the hospital and they've been able to give him something. They're wonderful and kind, the doctors. But I'm that frightened.'

'I'll be there as soon as I possibly can, Mam. Just hang on. Are you in the phone box?'

'Yes, dear. The phone box in the hospital, that is. The police came and fetched me and our Denise — ' Her voice broke.

Denise's voice took over, oddly grown up.

'She's upset. Dad's that poorly.'

'I know,' Rob soothed her. 'I'm going to get on the first train to Yorkshire, Denise. Can you and Mam look after each other until I get there?'

153

'Of course.' And then the call was interrupted by the pipping noise that warned the caller that their money was running out.

As if in slow motion, he replaced the handset and turned. Sylvana waited in the doorway, Elena on her hip, dark expressive eyes searching his.

'Something has happened to your father?' Her bottom lip quivered. 'Come upstairs and get changed while I pack your bag and you tell me. Papa, please telephone for Rob a taxi to the train station. Mamma, can you look after Elena for me?'

'Yes, yes.' Rita put out her arms and Elena swung into them with a beaming baby smile. Gwann patted Rob's arm before turning to the phone.

And then Sylvana's cool hand was in his.

'Come on, Rob.'

She urged him up the passages and stairs to their rooms where she pulled his khaki kitbag from on top of the wardrobe and began folding shirts.

'Can you tell me? Is it very bad?'

Automatically, he fumbled into clean clothes as he recounted everything his mother had said. He was shocked to notice that his hands were trembling.

Sylvana paused in her packing to fasten his shirt buttons for him.

'Poor William.' Her eyes were huge and soft. 'You go to him, and your mum and Denise, straight away. Give to him my love and a hug from Elena.'

'I'll telephone you as soon as I know anything.' Shirt finally buttoned, he reached for his tie. But, instead, he found himself dragging Sylvana into his arms, hugging her, hard, seeking comfort.

She hugged him back without any hesitation.

'I'll be here.'

Sylvana went with Rob in the taxi to Southampton Central railway station, clutching the railway timetable from Gwann's desk. Rob looked so shocked. He said little but his eyes spoke for him: he was frightened for his dad. She wanted to take that first step of the journey with him, to offer the silent support of her hand linked with his on the cold red vinyl of the back seat.

She flicked a discreet glance at her watch. Twenty minutes to go and all around them were lines of traffic. The wheels of the taxi had hardly turned in the last ten minutes. If Rob missed this train there would be another agonising thirty minutes to wait for the next and a much longer wait in London for the connecting train to Leeds.

As if reading her mind, Rob jerked forward and rapped on the window behind the driver.

'This is stupid. I can see the station from here and I can run faster than you can drive. Let me out here and just take my wife home, please.' He planted a swift kiss on Sylvana's lips, threw open the taxi door, pulling his kitbag with him, called, 'Bye, love!' and was gone, running easily and evenly beside the rows of traffic, his kitbag balanced on his shoulder.

'Traffic's fierce today,' the driver observed.

Tears

Once home, as they discussed the bad news, Sylvana was aware of speculative glances from her parents. The past few uneasy days had crackled with tension and Rob's homecoming had been spoiled. She was aware that she hadn't even asked how he'd left things with his commanding officer or how soon he could free himself for the Canadian job and what might happen in the meantime.

The Army didn't release its soldiers just because they decided to hand in their uniform, she realised that, and now she wished that she'd unbent enough to ask, to discuss the processes and possibilities calmly. It wasn't that they'd quarrelled, exactly, but there was a wariness between them.

She'd set it aside in a heartbeat on hearing Gwann's words to Rob, as she'd come downstairs, and then Rob's side of the telephone conversation. At that instant, her husband's needs had been paramount — he was in trouble and needed support, both emotionally and practically.

But now that he was gone and the urgency of the situation gone with him, she felt adrift again. The trouble with not asking questions was that she hadn't received any answers.

To occupy herself, she said, 'Come, Elena, you can help me peg out the washing.' Out in the long back yard, she found something comforting about the clean laundry smell and Rob's shirts flapping beside her smaller blouses and Elena's tiny shorts. The breezy summer's day was perfect for drying.

'I help,' Elena demanded, putting herself in charge of the pegs, as sweet as a fairy-tale princess with the basket over her little arm and her curls jiggling. Laughing, despite her worries, Sylvana turned at the sound of the back gate opening.

'Ian! Hello.'

Ian smiled, his long hair lifting from his collar in the wind.

'Is Gwann in?'

'He's cleaning down the restaurant kitchen after lunch, I think.'

Ian didn't make a move towards the house but grinned at Elena instead.

'And how are you, missy? You gave everybody a scare last week.'

Elena giggled up at Ian as if scaring her family were a great joke.

Sylvana frowned.

'She's not as healthy as I would like. She still wheezes. I saw the doctor and he said her asthma is because she gets new teeth. He has given her more medicine.'

Ian clicked his tongue in concern and, instantly, Elena tried to make the same noise, slapping her lips and frowning in concentration.

Turning back to pegging out her laundry, Sylvana waited for Ian to lounge off towards the kitchen door. Instead he lingered, following her movements with his eyes.

'So,' he said eventually. 'Elena's daddy must have had a shock, to come home and find his little girl in hospital.'

Shuddering at the unpleasant memory, Sylvana nodded.

'Of course.'

'Now that Rob's back, I suppose you'll be moving soon? You must be looking forward to having your own home again. Where will he be stationed?'

Suddenly, Sylvana found her eyes prickling with tears.

'I — I don't know what will happen yet.' She studied the stitching on a damp skirt so that Ian couldn't see her face.

He moved a step closer.

'Sylvana — I hope I'm not intruding. It's just that . . . I know not all wives are happy to see their husbands after a long absence.'

The remark hung delicately in the air. Sylvana found it difficult to swallow her tears, translate and understand Ian's words.

And then he was right beside her, so close that if she moved her hand just a little bit it would be in his.

'Sylvana, if I thought there was any chance . . . '

Oh! Her cheeks burned with horrified dismay. That's what Ian meant! Without looking at him, she pasted on a smile and stepped sharply to the side, rushing to peg out the last couple of things.

'I have jobs to do. I'll tell Papa that you are looking for him.'

She hurried indoors, heart racing, laundry basket swinging from one hand and Elena clutching the other, astounded that it had taken only a momentary silence from her to prompt Ian to begin a sentence that she hadn't wanted him to finish.

What on earth was he thinking of?

And if Ian thought that, then what kind of message would it send out if she stayed with her parents whilst Rob went to Canada?

Time Is Of The Essence

Rob stared at his father's face, half-hidden in bandages and gauze. At present, it was thought that he might have some vision, but it was essential that the eyes were kept as still as possible, the doctors said, so William's eyes were completely covered. They'd know more in a few days.

The hospital was quiet. Voices were hushed, footsteps muffled. William was sleeping, as he had done a lot since the accident, numbed by what he referred to as 'knock-out drops'. Whenever he was awake they'd all chat in reassuring tones to help him pass the time. His only other entertainment was to listen to the hospital radio.

Rob had only just completed his dash home to Yorkshire when the doctors decided to transfer William to Moorfields Eye Hospital in London as an emergency. Having changed trains in London, it would have been easy to feel frustrated that he had to turn around and traipse straight back, but he was just glad to be there to help Mam and Denise. Mam, especially, so white and tearful and shaky. Denise was glad to see him but withdrawn and silent compared to her usual bouncy self.

He'd tried to be positive, putting his arm around his mother's shoulders and saying, 'At least he's in the right place.'

Ida had accepted his hug but said dismally, 'Aye, but they can't work miracles.'

And with the doctors speaking gravely of retinal tears, corneal damage and time being of the essence, Rob could hardly pretend there was nothing to worry about, especially now the three of them were sitting silently with their bags at their feet, waiting for William to begin his transfer to the waiting surgeons in London.

'Are you sure you'll be all right in the ambulance with Dad?'

'I'll have to be.' Ida's voice was no more than a whisper. 'There isn't room for anyone else.'

'But I could go with Dad and you could go in the car with Denise.'

Ida managed a watery smile.

'No. I'll go with your father. You go with Denise. It's good of RBB Batteries to pay for a taxi all that way, isn't it? And for hotel rooms. Must be costing them a pretty penny.'

'Good?' Rob retorted. 'There's been an industrial accident and I'm glad they're facing up to their responsibilities. It would have been even better if they'd got Dad's protective glasses replaced.'

'But he sat on them, love.'

Rob took a breath. There was no point in worrying his mother with culpability and negligence now. So he squeezed her hand and played it her way.

'You look after Dad, then, and I'll look after Denise.'

★ ★ ★

In the car, Rob studied his sister's profile.

'If this had to happen, then I'm glad it was whilst I was in the country. At least I can help Mam a bit.'

Denise nodded, staring out of the window as the city gave way to countryside.

'Yes. I'm glad you hadn't gone to Canada.' She managed a smile. 'But I'd still be here for her and Dad, so that's something.'

He slid a comforting big-brotherly arm around her.

'I know you would have been.'

She was quiet for much of the journey but the moment she was reunited with Ida at the forbidding bulk of Moorfields Eye Hospital, Denise put on a brave face, giving Ida a big hug.

'How did Dad get on? Did he sleep much? Phew, this might be a special hospital but it smells just like an ordinary one, doesn't it?'

Ida laughed, but, red-eyed and pale, she looked as if she could just as easily have had a good cry.

'I'm sure they're marvellous folk, Denise. Let's hope so because Dad's operation is tonight.'

They waited out the time together in the hotel, drinking tea and watching a grainy colour television — the first any of them had ever seen — in the

165

residents' lounge until, at last, it was time for Rob to shut himself into the telephone cubicle in the foyer and ring the hospital for news. When he pushed his way out, a few minutes later, he didn't feel much wiser.

'They say that he's resting comfortably and that everything went exactly as expected,' he reported to his paper-white mother. 'They'll know more in a few days.'

'Oh, my,' Ida said faintly, clutching Denise's hand. 'Have we to wait till then?'

A Word In Your Ear

After three days of travelling between the hospital and the quiet but comfortable hotel organised by RBB Batteries, Ida was much calmer and more composed when they went to meet William's surgeon, Mr Dyment, in a grey jacket and a green tartan bow tie, at William's bedside.

166

Mr Dyment was so cautious that he made Rob want to shake information out of him but, finally, he got to the point.

'I'm optimistic, but I want him to stay as he is for another few days. There's quite a long road ahead, of course, and I'd like to put off assessing his sight until Tuesday.' With an apologetic smile, the doctor whisked off to his next patient.

Chilled by the lack of positive news, Rob asked, 'How do you feel about that, Dad?'

William's eyebrows moved above his eye patches.

'It's better than it could have been. Better than knowing the worst, but I can't deny that I'd be happier if the doctor had been a bit less careful about what he said. What's the matter with your mother?'

Rob glanced over to where Ida was snuffling into a tissue, Denise's arms around her.

'She's having a few tears, Dad. It's a

strain for her, too.'

William smiled and held out his hand in the direction of his wife.

'Why, you daft woman! Come here a minute.'

Ida slid her arms around William as best she could and rested her head on his shoulder.

'I'm not daft — just worried!'

Rob touched his sister's arm.

'Come on. Let's leave Mam and Dad alone for a few minutes. We'll go to the cafeteria.'

But Denise, too, burst into tears the moment she got outside the door.

'Sorry!' She sobbed. 'I'm imagining all the very worst things.'

Rob sat her at a table in a corner and fetched them a steaming pot of tea for two and a plateful of scones.

'I spoke to Sylvana on the phone last night. We think it would be a good idea if I took you down to Southampton for a bit. There's plenty of room above the restaurant and Rita and Gwann would love to see you. It's an anxious time and there'll be a lot more hospital visiting.'

Denise wiped her eyes.

'I don't mind hospital visiting.'

He shrugged.

'It's up to you. I thought it might be easier for Mam, now she knows her way around, if she knew you were with me and Sylvana for a few days. We'll have to put Mam and Dad first, won't we?'

Denise's wide gaze became thoughtful.

'Putting them first is a grand idea. Let's ask them.'

When Rob put the plan to his parents, Ida smiled.

'It would be a bit of a relief, Denise, if you'd like to stay with Sylvana's family. I was worried that you'd be bored to death hanging around the hospital.'

'I wouldn't,' Denise said. 'But I'll go with Robert, if you want. I'd love to see Sylvana and Elena. But only till Tuesday?'

'Definitely,' Rob assured her. 'We'll both come back on Tuesday.'

'That's settled, then,' William said. 'Robert, I'll just have a little word with you before you take Denise off, please.'

When Ida and Denise had gone off to fetch their coats, Rob moved to the bedside.

'I'm here, Dad.'

William groped for Rob's hand with his own warm, workworn one, reminding Rob of how he'd always gone to his dad with broken toys and those large, square hands had so often found a way to fix things.

'Thanks for taking Denise off your mam's hands, lad. She's had an awful shock and she'll relax if she knows Denise is safe with you.' He hesitated, then cleared his throat. 'I know you want to go off to Canada, and I understand you've always been one for new horizons and a life full of change. But I don't want you to talk to your mam about it now, while she's got so much on her mind. OK?'

'OK.' Rob found his voice suddenly hoarse.

'Thing is, you see, with the cost of airfares, and I won't be able to work for a long time . . . Well, she thinks that if you go to Canada she'll never see you again, because it won't be only for a set length of time, like an Army posting. So just keep it buttoned, lad, for now.'

'Yes, Dad,' Rob whispered.

Feeling like he'd been reproved, though his father hadn't so much as raised his voice, he went back into the corridor. As soon as Ida saw him, she glanced at her daughter.

'You just pop in and say goodbye to your dad, love.'

Rob looked down into his mother's worried face, waiting. She didn't leave him waiting long.

'Robert, just while your dad's so poorly, can you not mither him with talk about Canada? He thinks that if you go, we'll not be able to ever visit you — because he might not be able to work again. I know we'll find a way to get that airfare together but he's worried, so least said, soonest mended, eh?'

Rob rocked slightly on his heels.

'Are you saying you'd get on a plane

to Canada, Mam, to come and see me?'

Her eyes smiled.

'It can't be much worse than that London underground train, now, can it?'

A Picnic

Denise was back to her usual beaming self as she sat around the table in the family kitchen with Sylvana and Elena, Tereza, Gordon, Charles and Josie.

'This is lovely, like a little holiday.'

'I've got a new cricket bat and Charlie's got a cricket ball and stumps,' Gordon declared. 'Do you want to come to the park and play? We're not allowed to play in the yard because of the windows.'

'We could all go to the park,' Sylvana mused. 'Take a picnic?'

'Of course,' Denise agreed. 'But you'd better watch out. I can play cricket, you know. I'm from Yorkshire!'

Sylvana, watching Denise laughing

172

and joking with the children as the sandwiches and crisps were crammed into lunchboxes, found her hand suddenly enveloped in a large, warm one.

'Thanks, love,' Rob whispered. 'She's had such a shock and she needs something to take her mind off it. You and your family are just the tonic.'

Sylvana raised her eyebrows.

'I think she's more happy to be with her big brother than with us.'

He laughed softly, squeezing her fingers before letting her go.

'OK, we're all such great folk that being with us is all the consolation our Denise needs.'

Sylvana enjoyed strolling along the flagged pavement with her husband, her daughter, her niece and her nephews, the cries from the gulls sailing above them on the breeze combining with the laughter of the children spending their school holidays playing games in the street. The day was grey, but dry. When Sylvana thought how oppressively hot Malta would be in August, summer in

England didn't seem so bad. She pushed Elena's pram, Rob carried Josie on his shoulders and Denise and the boys raced ahead, carrying the cricket gear.

'It All Depends'

They'd already found a flat area of the park and set up stumps by the time Sylvana, Rob and the girls reached the gates. Rob grinned ruefully.

'I'm not sure whether I'm invited to play cricket with Denise. Our understanding of the rules has been known to differ.'

Sylvana smiled, almost shyly.

'I'd be glad to have your company. It can be tiresome to chase after two small girls who run in different directions.'

'I'll soon instil a little discipline in the troops,' Rob threatened. 'I'll teach them how to stand at attention and how to march!'

Sylvana laughed, but that was exactly

174

what Rob did, making the little girls giggle with his sergeant major act as the sun burned the clouds off to a haze and the cricketers got on contentedly with their match. It really was a lovely family occasion until she remembered poor William, and that Denise was only with them because of his bad luck. Perhaps Denise could come and spend holidays with them often, though . . .

She brought herself up short. She couldn't think about holidays when she didn't even know where they'd be living, but today wasn't the day to worry about that.

At lunchtime, Sylvana settled Josie and Elena with a sandwich each and Gordon and Charles ran up, puffing, with Denise alongside them, evidently having forgotten she was a young lady, wearing grass stains on her knees and a jumper around her waist.

'Sylvana, when Robert goes to Canada, can I still visit you and Elena?'

Sylvana didn't look up.

'We haven't made our plans yet.'

'But if he does, if Robert goes and you stay, I can visit you, can't I? And if Robert and you and Elena go, do you think your mum and dad will let me visit Tereza and the boys?'

Suddenly, Denise's eyes were bright with unshed tears.

'Let's not borrow trouble, Denise, eh?' Rob said quietly. 'Nobody's decided if and where anybody's going.'

On Tuesday, before he took Denise to catch the train, Rob made sure to spend some time with Elena. He intended to stay up in London for a few days and see for himself what his parents might need in the way of help.

But, all too soon, it was time to kiss both Elena and Sylvana goodbye.

'See you in a few days, love,' he murmured. 'I'll try not to be too long. But it all depends on what happens when the doctors take off those bandages.'

'I know.' Sylvana stroked his cheek. 'You stay as long as your parents need you.'

Good News

They made their way to William's ward. Rob's feet felt heavier with every step and he took Denise's arm as much to reassure himself as her. They had to ask at the nurse's station, as Ida had told them on the phone that William had been moved to a room further down the corridor. The nurse flipped quickly through her notes.

'William Denton. He's in room 3b but I'm afraid I have to ask you to wait for a few minutes. Your parents are with the doctor now.'

'Can't we go in?' Denise demanded, voice climbing.

The nurse smiled, but was firm.

'The doctor would prefer you to wait while he talks to your mother and father.'

'Thank you,' Rob said mechanically. They seated themselves on wooden chairs with red seats, and waited.

Patients walked past in dressing-gowns, nurses in uniform, doctors in white coats and orderlies in dark blue smocks. Wheelchairs. Trolleys of instruments, trolleys of plates and cutlery clinked past on their way back to the kitchens. Down the corridor, at the end, the door marked *3b* stood shut.

'What do you think?' Denise's voice was small.

'I just don't know, lovie. Let's try not to worry.'

After several more minutes, Denise took out a hankie and dabbed her eyes.

'They're being a long time.'

'They've got to do their job.' But he sighed. His heart had taken up a position in his boots.

Suddenly, the door to 3b opened and a doctor and a nurse came out. Talking in low voices, they disappeared into the next room.

Rob rose to his feet.

'Come on, then, before the nurse finds another reason to keep us out.' He ushered his sister along the corridor and with a heart thundering with apprehension, opened the door to his father's room.

By the bed, Ida sat, holding William's hand, her hankie screwed up in her hand.

William was propped up. He turned his head as they stepped through the door. The bandages were gone and the whites of his eyes were angry and red.

'Now, then, you two,' he said, after a moment. 'We were beginning to think you'd got lost.'

And with a surge of joy, Rob realised that his father was looking at him.

'You can see, Dad?' His voice wavered.

William held out his arms as Denise, unable to put on a brave front any more, charged across the room towards him.

'Oh, aye,' he answered, as if the subject had never been in doubt. 'Not ever so well, but the doctors say that it's going to get better and better. Early indications are good!'

Denise threw herself into his arms.

'Dad! I was frightened you were going to be blind.'

Stroking his daughter's hair, William beamed.

'No, I'm lucky.' He stretched out a hand to Rob. 'That surgeon is a very clever chap and I have him to thank for being able to see all the faces of those I love once again. Who could ask for more than that?'

Rob swallowed. He looked at mother, his father and his sister, all grinning through their tears.

'Nobody.'

Home At Last

When Rob returned to Southampton, it was almost a week later. He'd overseen his father's transfer back to the hospital in Leeds, got his mother and Denise settled in at home and made certain that they could get easily to and from the hospital by public transport, Ida never having learned to drive. Finally, he'd felt safe to embark on the long train journey back to Southampton.

Gwann was just opening up the restaurant when the taxi dropped Rob outside at six in the evening.

'Robert! You are home!' Gwann shook Rob's hand, his dark eyes glowing with pleasure. 'Come in. You are in time to eat dinner with Sylvana. Rita is bathing Elena and Josie. Sylvana is fetching the washing from the yard. Shall I shout?'

Robert felt quite strange, entering through the dining-room, like a customer. 'Thanks, Gwann, it's good to be back. But I'll find Sylvana — I know you're busy at this time of night.' He strode through the red and white dining-room, leaving behind the sounds of the restaurant kitchen rattling through the swing doors, into the hall, dropping his bag on the floor without pausing, through to the family kitchen. The room was empty but the back door stood open.

At the far end of the yard Sylvana stood in the late sunshine, unpegging and shaking out the clothes and folding them neatly into an oval wicker basket. He stepped outside, enjoying the oasis of calm, the birdsong and the sounds of children playing in nearby gardens as he strolled across the flagstones, anticipating that moment when Sylvana would see him and pleasure would flood her face.

'I'm Sorry'

He slowed when he realised that she was talking to someone and when he got to the other side of the sheets he saw that the someone was Ian, leaning his arms and chin on the top of the dividing fence.

'Yes, thank you, Elena is much better now. A new tooth is through and the wheezing, it has gone.'

Ian looked awkward.

'That's good. Um . . . Sylvana, if I spoke out of turn the other day, I'm very sorry.'

Rob halted.

Without looking at Ian, Sylvana snatched a pillowcase off the line and shook it hard.

'That is one of your English sayings, is it? I'm not sure I understand. But I would like to tell you that wherever my husband goes, I will go with him, me and Elena.'

A pause.

'OK,' Ian said. 'Thanks for telling

me.' Slowly, he turned away.

Rob waited, troubled. Sylvana. His wife. He wasn't sure precisely what he'd come in on the end of, but he had a fair idea. And what was clear was that valiant Sylvana had just put him first and made certain that Ian received the message loud and clear.

He waited until Sylvana, snapping the laundry into neat folds with irritated little movements, had progressed far enough up the washing-line to catch sight of him. She faltered, clutching one of his shirts to her.

'Oh! I didn't know you were there.'

He smiled, stepping close to take the shirt and drop it into the basket. Then he took her into his arms, warm and slender, and dropped a kiss on her nose.

'I think I'd like to stay in the Army. Would you like that?'

Suddenly, her dark eyes were shining and her face was alight with joy.

'Rob, really? I think I would love it!' She sobered for a moment. 'But what about the good job in Canada?'

He gave one last fleeting thought to the challenging work he'd been offered, out in the wide open spaces.

Important

'Home is where the heart is,' he admitted. 'Have you heard that English saying? It's become startlingly clear to me, this last week or two. Mam and Dad, in their different ways, they've made me think hard about who's important to me.

'So, wherever I go I'm going to do my best to see that you and Elena can be with me — all the time, not just two weeks out of every six, like with the Canadian job. I've done all that leaving my heart in one place while I'm in another. I want to be with you and I want to make you happy. And, for that matter, I want to be around for Mam and Dad and our Denise, too.'

Her arms tightened.

'So you think you'll get a UK posting?'

He threw back his head and laughed.

'I don't think the Army will dare offer me anything else! But if they do, Sylvana . . . '

'At least make them give you a posting so I can come, too.'

He kissed her, gently, softly.

'You bet. Let our home always be where our hearts are — together.'

We do hope that you have enjoyed reading this large print book.

Did you know that all of our titles are available for purchase?

We publish a wide range of high quality large print books including:
Romances, Mysteries, Classics
General Fiction
Non Fiction and Westerns

Special interest titles available in large print are:
The Little Oxford Dictionary
Music Book, Song Book
Hymn Book, Service Book

Also available from us courtesy of Oxford University Press:
Young Readers' Dictionary
(large print edition)
Young Readers' Thesaurus
(large print edition)

For further information or a free brochure, please contact us at:
Ulverscroft Large Print Books Ltd.,
The Green, Bradgate Road, Anstey,
Leicester, LE7 7FU, England.
Tel: (00 44) 0116 236 4325
Fax: (00 44) 0116 234 0205